Praise for Sophie Mouette

"Mouette handles the sizzling sex…with a generous hand….
[*Cat Scratch Fever*] is a delightful, amusing and sexy whodunit."
—*Romantic Times Book Reviews* (4 stars)

"This isn't erotica with a plot. This is an erotic romance within
a whodunit. And the result is a fabulously entertaining arousing work of erotic fiction with a very well developed plot and
strong characters. *Cat Scratch Fever* won't just arouse you, it
will divert you from the cares of your day."
—A Romance Review (4 roses)

"Sophie Mouette's 'Dyeing for Her' is a gloriously contemporary
piece of fiction."
—Erotica-Readers.com

Also by Sophie Mouette

Novels

The Hollywood Spice Series
Out of the Frying Pan
Love, in Stitches

Cat Scratch Fever
Possessed, Undressed, and in a Mess

Collections

Sexy in Your Stocking: Twelve Erotic Tales for the Holidays
Sexy With the Supernatural: Paranormal Lesbian Erotica
Sophie's Seductions: The BDSM Collection

Sophie's Seductions
THE BDSM COLLECTION

sophie mouette

LKP
LITTLE KISSES
PRESS

Sophie's Seductions: The BDSM Collection
Sophie Mouette

First Edition
ISBN-13:978-1-946462-03-9
ISBN-10:1-946462-03-9

Inquiries should be addressed to
Little Kisses Press
littlekissespress@gmail.com
http://www.littlekissespress.com

Cover image © sakkmesterke | Bigstockphoto.com
Cover and logo designed by Dayle Dermatis

Table of Contents

On His Honor

In the dark-paneled, high-ceilinged room, I heard the *tick-tick-tick* of fencing swords glancing off each other, accompanied by the occasional metallic swish. Once I entered from the locker room, I could also hear steady breathing behind the anonymous fencing masks, the slap of booted feet against the strip mats.

As I stretched, I watched Cameron, the club's top-seeded male fencer, winning point after point on his hapless opponent. Something about Cameron captivated me—and aroused me.

He was talented, and he was cocky. It's not always a great combination, but there's a level at which I like cocky. I like seeing how deep it goes, if the outer display of bravado hides an inner desire to be bested.

Once suited up for fencing, most people looked sexless. The loose, white canvas pants disguised curved hips or rounded asses, and the jackets did their best to make chests look flat—and for women, sports bras rarely accented the figure. The strap on the jacket that went between the legs muted telltale bulges.

Yet for a few, the outfits couldn't hide their shapes. Cameron was one. His rangy, graceful body, piercing dark eyes, and long dark ponytail hanging out from below his mask made him look like Musketeer material. It wasn't hard to imagine him in the plumed hat, fighting for the honor of Queen and Cardinal.

I leaned my hands against the padded wall and pointed my right leg back, pressing my heel into the floor and feeling the glorious stretch in my calf muscle.

Honor. It seems like an archaic concept to some, but in fencing, it's paramount. Competitions now require electronic scoring, with your sword wired to sense when the tip touches your opponent. But that's mostly for hard-to-call shots when there's less than a second between each epée touching the other person.

We practice here without electronics. It's one of the reasons I chose this club, chose Giulio Santorini as the fencing master who could push me to the limits of my abilities. Giulio demands honor, and anyone without it is summarily dismissed from his presence and the club.

Cameron had honor. I'd been watching him closely, and although he was a lightning-fast, ruthless fencer, he never called a shot he didn't think was valid, never failed to accept a shot he knew was a solid hit.

I grabbed my epée and went to work on point control. Standing before the wall, I chose a spot and lunged. The tip hit the exact spot, the whippy blade bending before I snapped back to a standing position.

In a competition, if you miss the shot during that lunge, you'd better be sure you can get back out of the way in less than a heartbeat.

Kind of like relationships. It pays to have a fast retreat, just in case.

I hadn't decided how Cameron felt about women. Oh, he wasn't gay. He strutted and preened around the ladies. He even had groupies, who came to competitions and fluttered from the sidelines. I was less clear on his attitude about women fencers. Competitions are segregated by gender, but practices can go either way.

The other fencers in the club had welcomed me, and knew that I was damn good. But so far, Cameron hadn't made any move to spar against me.

Or any other kind of move.

So, as usual, I took it upon myself to make the moves. That's why I was here on a Saturday evening. Giulio took weekends off, but we were free to come in and practice. I knew that Cameron did and tended to be the last one to leave.

I kept stretching until his opponent, sweaty and exhausted, headed to the locker room, and I waited for Cameron to approach, a magpie after a shiny toy.

I crossed my legs, then bent from the waist. I was limber enough to plant my hands flat on the floor. The bulky fencing outfit couldn't disguise my figure, either.

"Abby, isn't it?"

I'd been fencing here for almost a month, practicing up to five times a week. I suspected that he did know my name.

I bit back the smile that threatened to break free. He was like a teenage boy, trying to act cool in front of the girl he fancied. He had no idea that I saw right through him.

I straightened. "That's right," I said. "And you're Cameron, I believe."

When he saw that I wasn't going to swoon under his gaze, he changed his tack. Smart move. Never assume you can use the same successful attack over and over. Each opponent is different.

"I've been watching you," he said. (As if I didn't know. So far, he thought I was prey, and he the predator.) "You show a great deal of promise."

"I hope so," I said evenly. "I was the top seeded member of my last club." I named it, and saw the flicker of respect in his dark eyes.

"Perhaps we can spar sometime," he said.

Did he mean on the strip, or in the bedroom?

Which begged the question, did I want to fence him until we dropped from exhaustion or fuck him until we dropped from exhaustion?

The only issue was both had to be on my own terms.

Cameron might not like that.

If my *proclivities* didn't interest him, then we'd go no further. I had a feeling that he wasn't used to acquiescing, and the challenge intrigued me. Aroused me.

He didn't know that I was the predator, and he the prey. I the spider, and he the fly.

And I could weave a very sticky web.

"I could give you a few pointers," he went on.

I smiled then. "Or I could give you a few."

His nostrils flared at the challenge. I held my breath, waiting to see whether he'd pass this first test.

"You seem sure of yourself," he said.

"I am sure of myself," I said. "I'm not saying there isn't room for learning, but rather than a teaching session, I'm interested in a challenge."

He balanced the point of the epée on the toe of his soft boot and pressed down. The blade curved, twanged back into shape. "A challenge?"

"I enjoy fighting against the best," I said. "It brings out my best."

"You think you can beat me?" he asked.

Oh, I had him. He was intrigued. His ego was on the line. I homed in on the kill. "Maybe," I said. "But to make it interesting, let's wager on the outcome."

"Dinner?" His espresso eyes watched me with the same intensity he'd watch an opponent during a match. Good—he recognized that our match had already begun.

"I was thinking of something different." I watched his reaction as I spoke. "If I win, I get to do what I want with you for half an hour and you have to go along with it. If I lose, you get the same privilege. Could be cleaning my kitchen." I moved closer, where I'd be inside his guard if we were fencing. "Could be something more…personal."

Cameron's smile looked, if anything, a little cockier, but his eyes lost their focus briefly and his pupils widened, black overtaking the brown. I love that expression, a bit of panic and a whole lot of lust mixing together.

It's amusing as well as hot when the guy has the illusion he's still in control.

Cameron's answer showed he imagined he was. "The kitchen's the least interesting room in my house. We'll find someplace else for me to take advantage of my half-hour."

Actually, my kitchen could be very interesting, but "creative uses for wooden spoons" was a discussion for later.

"We should set ground rules," I said, more for his benefit than my own. "Nothing that could be truly harmful. And if the winner manages to pick the other person's worst nightmare, that counts as harm."

"Honor system that neither of us will invent phobias to get out of stuff." Cameron said it as a statement, not a question. "It has to really bother you to count. Otherwise you stick it out."

"Of course!" I forced myself to look away from Cameron for a second, back to the strip mats. The place was starting to clear out. "So, shall we?"

He bowed, an elegant courtier's gesture. I matched it, and we headed for the mats.

Beginners often think fencing is about speed or reach or grace. They're wrong. All of those are important, but the two key things are absolute control over your weapon and the ability to figure out your opponent's psychology.

Rather like sex, at least my kind of sex.

You can't really watch your opponent's eyes when you fence. The masks interfere. Instead, you learn to read other things. It wasn't hard to tell what Cameron hoped I would do.

Ideally that unspoken communication happens in sex, too. Of course, in sex, unlike fencing, you sooner or later try to give the other person what he wants.

For a while the world narrowed to the two of us and our epées. I could feel sweat clinging to me, soaking into my jacket and hair, but most of my attention was on Cameron's gorgeous body, which was simultaneously attacking and evading me just as skillfully as I'd expected, and on our efforts to symbolically kill each other.

Some might consider that an odd seduction, but those people aren't fencers.

At least we could get the stabbing each other in the heart bit out of the way right up front

In the heart, actually, was where I got him. He went for a head shot, which I parried, but he didn't snap back into his defense fast enough. He left me a lightning-fast opening.

A touch to the chest. Would it be enough? Some might claim it was too light.

He stopped in his tracks, lowered his blade with theatrical flair. "Very impressive, Abby. Thank you for such a challenging match."

There was a smattering of applause from the couple of people who were left, watching in their street clothes. After our bout ended they picked up their gear and headed out.

I locked the door behind them, then turned and winked at Cameron, who was gratefully stripping off his sweaty jacket.

"So, am I cleaning your kitchen?"

I laughed. "Do I look that dumb? Go take a shower and meet me out here." I went off to follow my own advice.

I knew he could run out on me as soon as my back was turned. I also knew he wouldn't.

By the time I emerged from the locker room, Cameron was waiting for me. I found myself strutting as I crossed the room. Tight black jeans, high-heeled Goth boots, a form-fitting forest green stretch velvet turtleneck and an appreciative audience put a little feline in my walk.

"I didn't know if I should get dressed or not, so I compromised." He gestured down his bare torso, where a few stray water drops gleamed. As if I hadn't already noticed the lovely view.

His lower body in snug, faded Levis and bare feet was a nice view, too, but I had plans for improving it.

"You're not going to need those jeans," I said casually. "Take them off." I could have softened it with a *please*, but I wanted to see how he reacted.

A look of confusion, then a catch in the breath and his pupils widening. This time he had no illusion he was in charge, but I couldn't tell yet how he felt about it. His hands fumbled for his zipper but his eyes stayed locked into mine as if he were scared to look away. No argument, though, just one gorgeous lanky boy slithering his jeans out of the way.

I'd anticipated the muscled legs, the sculpted ass, and they were just as fine as I'd pictured them. He hadn't bothered putting underwear on—or maybe he never wore it.

"Now that's a pleasant surprise," I said, circling my prey.

His cock twitched as if acknowledging the compliment.

The salle used to be a dance studio and a barre had been left on one wall for stretching. "Hold onto that barre with one hand," I ordered, "and don't let go until I tell you. And hold still unless I tell you it's all right to move."

I was glad I'd worn heels. I wouldn't have to use rappelling gear to kiss him.

I took advantage of that immediately, pressing my clothed body against his naked one. It made his status clear: The naked one is the toy. I emphasized it by running my hands over his body, playing special attention to his perfect buns, like warm velveted marble.

I felt him fighting the instinct to wrap his arms around me. I hadn't figured out what I'd do to him if he broke position, but I'd come up with something. I always did, because boys would break until they really accepted I was in charge. So far, though, Cameron was obeying.

Honor-bound.

Not being able to hold me wasn't keeping him from kissing me back. He used his tongue almost as skillfully as his sword. I could get to like that.

Too much, in fact. I could spend my half hour just kissing and touching him. It would be fun for both of us, but it wouldn't answer certain crucial questions.

I let go.

I went to my fencing bag, put my leather gloves back on, picked up my epée and returned to him. "The name of today's game is Don't Come. I'm going to do things to you that I hope you'll enjoy. But you're not to come until I say it's okay."

I placed the epée's guarded tip at the hollow of his throat, barely touching skin. I knew he could feel it, though. That's one of the most vulnerable points on the body, one that's usually protected by the mask and a gorget. "Do you understand?" I asked.

Small shivers darted over his skin. He licked his lips. "Yes, Abby," he whispered, his normally firm voice barely audible.

Something else, on the other hand, was looking damn firm.

"Yes, *my lady*," I said. He nodded and mouthed the words after me.

His eyes were dark as Starbuck's finest and blank as a blind man's. He was gone, losing himself in a place where he wasn't in control and that was just fine.

Cameron didn't telegraph a lot when he was fencing, but he was doing so now, and what he was telling me was that he was getting way into this.

Perfect.

I let the blade trail, making sure he could feel the cold metal against his chest, down his belly, snaking down his thigh. Cameron had been fencing at least as long as I had. He knew an epée was dull. But knowing that doesn't fend off that stubborn part of your brain that only registers a sword on your naked skin and wants to panic.

Or the nerve endings that feel the cold caress of metal and turn it into fire.

Some people find those warring impulses distinctly non-erotic. Cameron, on the other hand, squirmed and sighed. My kind of guy.

I ran the epée up his leg, let it rest briefly against his balls. This elicited a little moan.

I glanced up at the clock. Fifteen minutes left and I was just getting started. Damn, I should have asked for more time.

Reluctantly, I set the sword down.

Warm leather on hot skin. I've always thought there's nothing like it. I started on his nipples, a light touch to see if they were sensitive.

They were.

I pinched gently.

"Please," he hissed.

"Please no or please yes?"

"Please yes." And as I complied, he breathed, "Harder."

Oh yes. My kind of guy. But I couldn't let him get away with that almost-demand.

"Didn't you forget something?" I slapped his ass lightly, an application of warm leather on bare skin he hadn't been expecting. When he didn't answer immediately, I did it again, although I figured he wasn't answering because he'd momentarily lost higher brain function.

He figured it out on the third slap. "Please yes, my lady."

"Good boy." I gave him what he wanted: one nipple pinched and twisted and the other captured in my hot mouth.

My free hand reached between his legs, cupped his balls. One leather-clad finger teased that exquisitely sensitive spot at their base.

He was making the most interesting noises now, so I kept it up for a few minutes. Then I kissed my way down his body.

Some women with my tastes won't suck cock. Think it spoils a boy or something. I enjoy it way too much to pass it up: that first chance to smell that intimate flesh, to taste it, to feel that iron-peach sensation in my mouth. The power of feeling him quiver, wanting so badly to explode down my throat.

Then stopping and pulling back until he cooled down.

Repeat as needed, until he was in a sweaty panic.

He never stirred from the position I'd told him to hold. Once I thought I saw his hand twitch as if he wanted to put it on the back of my head, but he didn't.

My time was almost up. The obvious choices were to finish him off or to order him to attend to the growing puddle in my panties.

I chose a third path. "Doing okay?" I asked, rising and lightly stroking his face.

"Oh yeah!" His voice was far away but not lost. Found, even.

"Ready to come?"

"Yes, my lady." It seemed to fall so naturally from his lips. "Please? That's in your hands now, I guess."

I smiled. No, I smirked. "I'm putting it into your hands. Make yourself come for me, Cameron."

His free hand closed around his cock and began pumping. The hand on the barre never let go. He looked toward the wall, trying to hide in his own shoulder.

I turned his face forward. "Look at me, Cameron. Look in my eyes while you're coming for me."

His face flared red, but he obeyed.

And seconds later, he grunted out a string of curses as he came all over the floor.

At which point, I echoed him—a mini-gasm, but not bad for no hands.

"How about a rematch later in the week, my lady?" he asked as soon as he caught his breath.

"Half hour's up. You can call me Abby again."

"Abby," he repeated, as dutifully as he'd called me "my lady." He wouldn't forget my name now. I thought he looked a little disappointed. Better and better.

We made a date for Wednesday evening. He offered to carry my fencing bag to the car, but I declined.

"You should clean that up before you leave," I tossed over my shoulder as I walked away. I had no doubt that he would.

*

By Wednesday evening, I was buzzing with the combination of adrenaline and arousal.

We'd already agreed on the terms. A full half-hour of fighting, with the person winning the most points winning the match. Winner took the loser home and kept them 'til midnight.

As I changed into my gear, the question in my mind was: What did he truly want, deep down? Did he want to win so he could turn the tables on me? Or did he want me to win, because he craved finding out how much farther I would take him? If the latter, would he let me win?

I hoped not. I respected honor more than anything.

As I walked into the salle, I took a deep, steadying breath. It would do me no good to let my imagination distract me from the bout. My own honor demanded I give him my best, too.

Cameron emerged from the men's locker room as I was stretching. He gave me a lazy salute, and I nodded. I warmed up with a few of my regular sparring partners, and then we were ready to begin.

We had an audience again—five or six people who abandoned their own practice and settled onto the bleachers to watch. News of our previous match had made its way through the club. We hadn't advertised this one, but as soon as people figured out we were going to spar, they wanted to watch.

The nice thing was that we were able to ask someone to keep score for us. As it turned out, we needed it.

We were both in rare form. I don't know if I'd ever seen Cameron move so swiftly, so gracefully. Even if he wanted me to win, he wasn't going to make it easy for me.

Good.

The world narrowed to my opponent and me, to the strip, to the sound of my own heart pounding and the feel of the slender blade I controlled.

I lunged a hair too far, and didn't pull back as fast as I normally could, and he made a solid hit. We stepped apart, saluted again, and started over. This time I went for a strong attack, pressing him back. His retreat along the strip was graceful, his parries solid, not letting me in for a winning shot.

The next bout, we saluted, then neither of us moved. Fencing is often compared to chess—you have to gauge your opponent, see many moves ahead of them. Sometimes it's a stand-off. If you move first, you've already left yourself open.

This time, I outlasted him. Maybe he got to thinking about what was at stake. But when he changed stance and thrust, I was already moving. My epée shot out and connected squarely on his chest.

And on it went. I was so intent on the match that I almost didn't hear the call announcing that the half-hour was up. The voice sounded distant, muffled.

We stripped off our masks and waited for the tally. I was breathing heavily, the sweat trickling down my face. It had been a good match, either way.

But I hoped I'd won. My stomach tightened, and I couldn't look at him.

The tally was announced: I'd beat him by one point.

"Well fought," he said, shaking my hand. Although his face remained impassive, I saw the look in his eyes, one I liked very much.

"See you outside in twenty minutes," I murmured, just to him. "You'll follow me home."

*

When we got to my home, I pointed to the teak coffee table.

"There's a questionnaire on there for you," I said. "I know you'll be honest in your answers. Fill it out—neatly."

"Yes, my lady," he said promptly.

I didn't let him see my eyebrow raise. I was impressed: He was falling into the role quite nicely.

I had a basic idea of how the evening would go, but I'd wait to make final plans until after I'd seen his responses to the questionnaire. First on the schedule, in any case, was a little fun for myself.

I'd discovered how talented his tongue was for kissing. The first order of business was to put it to use elsewhere.

To that end, I put on a simple, teal-blue satin camisole that brushed the tops of my thighs. While there's something to be said for leather and spiked heels, I'd rather reinforce my status with actions and words than outfits that teeter on the brink of cliché. Sometimes a unexpected look keeps my prey nicely off-balance.

Besides, I wanted to be comfortable. I was hoping for a long night of carnal inventiveness.

I took my time, giving him ample chance to finish the questionnaire. I'd included every variation and kink I could think of; no doubt some of them would intrigue him, some would be a definite turn-off, and some would give him pause for consideration.

When I entered the living room, he was sitting on the floor by the coffee table, chewing on the end of the pencil. He hadn't even sat on the sofa, as if he knew he'd have to ask permission for that.

Oh my, this boy was a natural. I was amazed nobody had snapped him up yet, and thrilled that I'd been the first to tap into his submissive tendencies.

I felt that thrill all the way down to my clit.

He looked up as I walked in. His nostrils flared at the sight of me.

"I'm sorry, my lady, but I'm not quite finished."

"Take your time," I said. "It's important, and there's no penalty for taking too long."

I poured myself a glass of crisp Chardonnay. I wouldn't drink much, but it could serve as a nice prop.

I had settled myself into an armchair and taken a few sips when he rose to his knees and presented the questionnaire to me like a royal coronet on a pillow.

"Thank you, Cameron." I set the wine down and accepted the pages. "I'm going to take my time reading this, so for starters…strip."

I didn't look up until I sensed he was kneeling in front of me again. Then I slowly raised my eyes over the paper and regarded him.

Oh, he was lovely. That slender but muscular chest, the whipcord arms, the firm thighs. He was approaching hardness, not quite fully erect.

"While I'm reading, we'll start with you massaging my feet. You may lick them if you want, but since I don't know if you're interested in that, you have the option not to. If you have a question, you may say, 'my lady?'; otherwise, don't talk. Understood?"

"Yes, my lady."

"Carry on, then."

I perused his answers. He showed strong interest in bondage and pain play, with some reservations. Fair enough. I might be able to push those boundaries later, but I'd pay attention.

His hands worked magic on my feet, pressing on the right places with strokes firm enough not to tickle. When his tongue snaked in between my toes, I hid my smile behind the questionnaire. God, it felt so good!

I turned a page.

"You may lick my calves and work your way up my thighs."

According to the survey, he wasn't sure about anal play. Fine, we could discuss that later, too.

I spread my legs, allowing him access farther up between my legs. I know he could smell my musky scent now—goodness knows I was wet. He started to get close, then hesitated.

"Very good, Cameron," I said. "You knew you didn't have permission yet."

His tongue trailed spirals high up on my inner thighs. Then, "My lady?"

"Yes, Cameron?"

"May I?"

"Yes, Cameron, you may."

I'm sure the papers rattled a little when his tongue swiped across my clit. Like his hands, his tongue moved in firm strokes. He spent some time lapping at my cunt, tasting me, using his tongue like a tiny cock to press inside me.

I skimmed the last page of the questionnaire, which listed some hardcore stuff we wouldn't do tonight anyway, then dropped the pages. It was time to enjoy myself.

I grabbed his long dark ponytail, running my fingers between it and dividing into two, like reins. When I tugged, I heard him let loose with a breathy moan that vibrated into my cunt, and he redoubled his efforts.

So, he liked that? Good.

I used his hair to direct him, and, when I finally pushed his head harder against me, he picked up the cue perfectly. His tongue whipped across my clit like a sword, faster and harder. Dimly I was aware that he'd kept his hands on his knees, as if knowing I hadn't given him permission to touch me except with his mouth.

That realization helped tumble me over the edge.

I kept his face pressed against me for a moment, then released some of the pressure. He responded by laving gently with the flat of his tongue, tasting my juices. My thighs quivered, and I held him there until I'd recovered my composure.

Then, my hands still entwined in his hair, I pulled him so he was kneeling up. I think it surprised him when I pulled him close and kissed him.

Hell, it surprised me a little, not so much the kiss itself as the wave of sweet possessiveness that washed over me as I devoured his mouth.

I've had my share of play partners. Most of them probably figured I was the least romantic woman on earth. I didn't "date" those guys. I topped them, I fucked them, we had a hot, sweaty time together, and it never got more complicated than that.

Deep down, though, I *am* a romantic. Except I'm not looking for a white knight. I want to be the knight—or perhaps the queen—who protects, controls, and cares for my beloved vassal, and punishes him in my dungeon when need be. (Which would be whenever we both thought it would be fun.)

Sophie Mouette

It had never happened, though. The right "vassal" had to be more than hot and submissive. I wanted strength, intelligence, shared interests outside the bedroom, and most of all, shared values. Archaic ones like *honor* and the importance of one's word.

Damn if I wasn't picturing Cameron in that role. Not a slave, but a knight in his own right, sworn to my service.

I was jumping the gun badly. Tonight I only had until midnight, and then he was free to go.

Unless he decided he didn't want to.

I put my hand on his chest, pushed him away, and stood. "I think we'll be more comfortable in the bedroom now."

"My lady?"

"Yes?"

"Do I walk? Or..."

The question zinged right to my groin. I hadn't planned to tell him to crawl, but the tone of Cameron's voice, his lowered eyes, and most of all, his quivering cock told me he craved it.

And he'd look so charming doing it, with his cat's grace.

I smiled, trying to put all the evil and tenderness I feeling into it. "Hands and knees."

He took a deep breath, closed his eyes, flushed. Then he sank to all fours and for a second rested his head against my calf.

"Follow me." I led him into the bedroom, glancing back frequently to enjoy the view.

My bedroom's nothing that unusual, although I do have restraint points attached to the bed. What made him whistle was the collection of whips and floggers hung artistically on the wall. They ranged from the merest caress of fur and light suede to a singletail I didn't have room to use indoors. An antique umbrella stand held canes of varying weights.

"Yes?" I said. "What do you think?"

"I'm impressed, my lady. And nervous."

And, I noted, hard enough to pound nails.

"Anything especially exciting? Or scary?"

He pointed to the singletail as scary. Smart boy. Someone skilled can flick the petals off a rose without bruising them, but used carelessly, a singletail is a weapon.

Somewhat to my surprise, he mentioned canes as something that intrigued him. "I read a collection of Victorian porn back in college," he confessed. "Someone's getting caned—and loving it—every five pages. I've been fantasizing ever since, my lady."

Honesty compelled me to say, "Canes can leave marks."

"I know, my lady. But a couple of stripes…would be worth it."

I could have tied him up. Instead, I bent him over the foot of the bed and told him, on his honor, not to move.

Not moving when your butt is on fire takes fortitude. Even if the pain transmutes to pleasure almost immediately, instinct tells you to flinch away. This time, however, I wanted him to choose with each stroke to obey and stay put, choose to ride the pain through to pleasure.

I put my leather gloves on and ran my hands along his body, letting him feel the leather against his skin.

Then I began to spank.

I started softly, a sensuous rhythm of light taps to bring a flush to his skin. He relaxed into it quickly, making noises of pleasure with each impact. As his ass flushed pink, I put more snap into the blows, syncopated the rhythm so he didn't know what to expect.

So far, Cameron was showing every sign of enjoying himself. Some of his noises were clearly gasps of pain, but most sounded like pure pleasure and his cock glistened with precome.

"Ready for something more intense?" I asked.

He nodded.

I buried my fingers in the hair on the back of his neck. "Answer me, Cameron. Say it, or you won't get it."

Making an obvious effort to remember English, he whispered, "Yes, my lady. I am." Then, not as an afterthought, but as if he needed a pause for breath, he added, "Please."

I kissed his shoulder and whispered, "You're doing great."

Then I reached for a medium-weight deerskin flogger, one with both thud and sting, and let it snap.

I was rewarded by a sharply indrawn breath, a gasp, and a barely audible, "Thank you."

He should have said "Thank you, my lady," but I wasn't going to quibble. Not when the sound of his thanks left me with juices dripping down my leg.

Ten more strikes with that flogger, and a thanks drawn from his lips by each one. I stopped after that. Cupping his buns in my gloved hands, I could feel their throbbing heat even through the leather.

Keeping my hand in contact with his skin, I walked up so I could see his face.

The Cameron of the salle was gone, all the cockiness missing. He looked younger and curiously innocent with his flushed face, but at the same time Pan-like, timeless and ecstatic and filled with dark wisdom.

"More?"

"Please, my lady. Thank you." I had to strain to hear him, but his face answered the question better than any words could.

Something harsher this time, braided falls with small, stinging knots on some of them.

He keened with each stroke, a litany of *yes* and *thank you* and *my lady*. Not much sense, just music that fit the dance of the lash.

I like inflicting pain, but only when someone embraces it. Cameron did more than embrace it. He was letting it take him on a journey to a place he'd never been before. And he was taking me along for the ride.

I was almost scared myself to take the next step. Basically it was a caning, something I'd done many times to other men, but this seemed more intimate, less like play and more like a ritual. I'd imagined the act, or something like it, from the first time I caught a glimpse of something receptive behind Cameron's strength.

I hadn't imagined what would be going through my mind in the moment—a courtly scene, the liege striking her knight with a sword to bind him to her service.

When I'd imagined it, I hadn't really imagined Cameron, just his body.

Now that I knew more about him, it was irresistible.

I set down the whip, caressed his ass again, went to my fencing bag.

Took out the epée.

I brought it over so he could get a good look at it. "Do you know why I have this?"

"You're going to cane me with it, my lady."

"Very good. Do you know why?"

"Because you'll enjoy it."

"Because *we'll* enjoy it," I corrected. "But that's not the only reason. I'm going to hit you with this because the epée brought you to me. The epée and your honor and your skill, because I wouldn't have been interested in you if you weren't who you are."

I moved the blade closer to his lips. He knew what to do.

I positioned myself behind him, pulled it back, whipped it down hard onto the bed next to him. He jumped, laughed nervously. While he was still twitching, I struck him for real.

He muffled a scream as a red welt blossomed.

If I'd wanted to be cruel, I'd have repeated it immediately. Instead, I waited for the sharp pain to shift to pleasure. I leaned forward, watching as his face transformed, the tight determination to endure changing to a dazzled smile. "Again?" I asked.

I didn't correct him this time when he only nodded. There are times you can't expect someone to speak.

"I'm going to mark you with this, Cameron," I crooned. "I'm going to leave you something so you'll remember that while you may win sometimes in the salle, you will yield to me when I ask it in private." I didn't really know where the words were coming from. They just poured out.

"Yes, my lady, I will. I swear."

Twice more, I pulled the blade back and brought it down like a cane across his ass.

By the third blow, his breath was coming in sobbing gasps. He wasn't using a safe word or begging for mercy—if anything, his little gasps of "Please" sounded like "Please go on." But I judged he'd had enough.

I set the epée down, crawled onto the bed and pulled Cameron down next to me. I folded him in my arms while he floated on his endorphin high. *Mine*, I thought contentedly, possessively.

I didn't realize I'd said it out loud until he responded, almost soundlessly, "Yours."

"Until midnight," I corrected, glancing at the clock. Almost eleven. I hoped to end the night with a fuck, a pleasure we both deserved, but the first order of business was talking with him a little to make sure he was really all right. "Then you're free to go."

"But am I free to stay? Please, my lady?"

My heart clenched. "Do you know what you might be getting yourself into?"

I propped myself up on one elbow so I could watch his face as he thought about how to answer.

"Not exactly, my lady," he finally admitted. "For tonight, anything you'd like, and then omelets for breakfast. Or eggs Benedict if you prefer. After that, I'm sure you'll tell me."

"For one thing," I said, "you did this unusual parry in the second bout. I'd like you to show me how you did it."

"As you wish, lady. As long as you don't use it against me in the future."

I grabbed his hair again, pulled his head back so he was looking into my eyes. "Silly boy," I whispered. "Of course I will. If you're not out of here by midnight, I'll use everything you have against you. And you'll love it."

"Yes, my lady," was all he managed to say before I stopped his foolish talking with a kiss.

Don't Move

Hell, yes," I said, when Emily pointed to a picture of a bound woman and asked if I thought she looked hot.

"Could we try that sometime?" she wondered next, I had to try so hard not to sound like an overexcited teenage boy that all I managed to get out was, "Really?" Emily's words, Emily's unexpected request to try something new and a bit kinkier than our usual fare hit me like some kind of drug rush. Bottle this feeling and I'd be rich.

"Really. At least...I think so," she said. "Don't you think she looks hot like that?" She waved the picture at me again.

The short answer, which I gave her, was *hell yes*. Wrist-to-thigh cuffs held the pretty model's hands in place by her sides, and her legs were cuffed at the ankles, spread wide, and then obviously tethered to something not visible in the picture. It was in our favorite sex-toy catalogue, so the model's sex was discreetly covered by PVC panties, but under the shiny black covering, she had to be open, ready to be eaten or fucked.

Eager for it, according to my imagination.

It was a great image, made even lovelier by substituting my girlfriend for the model. Emily's long red hair would be tousled and tangled from writhing within her bonds—playfully pretend-struggling that was really squirming in pleasure—her skin sleek with sweat, her pussy slick and dripping, ready for me.

The idea shot straight from my brain to my cock, which twitched toward erection at record speed.

"I'd love to," I told her, pulling her (catalogue and all) onto my lap so I could press my hardening dick against her and let her feel how much I liked it. "You'd look beautiful like that. And I'd love having you at my mercy like that. Helpless, unable to resist." I caressed her breasts through her tank top until her nipples popped out, dark and stiff behind the thin, light blue fabric. Returning the favor, she made small circles with her shorts-clad butt, teasing at my erection.

"I couldn't," she purred. "Resist, that is. I'd be all open and wet and you could do anything you wanted to me." Then she giggled and, turning, kissed the end of my nose. "Not like I resist you all that much anyway, but I really like the idea of giving you control once in a while. Been working up the nerve to talk about it for a while and the picture gave me a prop to use. But…"

Her voice trailed off, and she stopped moving. I could feel her body tense, and not in a good way.

"But?" I put my arm around her.

"But at the same time it's scary," she admitted. "Not the giving-up-control part. I trust you, and I think that could be a lot of fun. But I've never actually been tied up, and…what if I freak?"

"Is this something like your thing with planes?"

She muttered an almost inaudible "Yeah." It wasn't exactly fear of flying that kept Emily on the ground; it was the feeling she was trapped on the plane. If someone had issued her a parachute and told her she could jump out anytime, though, I think she'd have been fine.

"So you wanted to feel controlled—but not necessarily confined?"

She nodded eagerly.

Hmm, worked for me. Sexy as the bands of leather looked against the model's skin, and fun as it might be to tie Emily up in some theoretical world where she wasn't claustrophobic, what I really found arousing was the idea of a woman voluntarily open and helpless to my whim, with or without bondage. And that gave me an idea.

But then Emily turned in my lap until she was straddling me, rocked forward, pulled her shirt off...and somehow we didn't get around to trying my idea that afternoon, but did test the limits of that particular chair in some interesting ways.

I think she thought I'd forgotten the conversation. But I hadn't.

I just let it go for a few days until I got everything worked out in my mind, and picked up a few props.

Tonight, as we headed to the bedroom, I told her, generally, what I had in mind, and had the pleasure of watching her eyes get wide and kind of glazed with anticipation.

Sweet.

Once we got naked, and I asked Emily—no, told her—to lie on her back on the bed. She grinned dreamily as she lay down.

Out of my bag of tricks I first pulled a pair of black leather cuffs. They weren't bondage cuffs, but just plain bands with studs like a rocker would wear onstage. I made sure she could see that there was no way to attach them to anything before I buckled them around her wrists.

"My God, you look sexy," I said. "The dark leather against your pale skin. I wish I'd found bigger ones for your ankles."

She lifted her hands and turned her wrists back and forth, admiring the cuffs.

"I didn't say you could do that," I said. I kept a little teasing note in my voice, figuring we'd lead up to things slowly.

I arranged her like the model in the picture, legs spread wide, a pillow under her butt so her pussy was even more exposed, hands on her thighs.

It was hard to go slow when she looked so damn hot.

"Don't move," I told her. "The game tonight is you hold still until I say it's okay to move."

She disobeyed immediately with a little squirmy shiver. It was cute and made her breasts jiggle enticingly, but I still shook my head and said, "Bad girl. Just for that, I won't touch you yet."

Instead I posed what I hoped was sexily at the foot of the bed, took my cock in my own hand, and began to stroke. I was already hard, just from looking at her, from how she allowed me pose her on the bed, from how she obeyed me now, unmoving except for breathing heavily as she fixed her gaze on my hand.

I thumbed the slick moisture from the tip of my cock and held it to her lips. She started to stick her tongue out, then stopped, remembering.

"Good girl," I said. "You may taste now."

I slipped my finger between her lips. She sucked eagerly, and I felt the sensation all the way down to my cock.

As tempting as it was to encourage her to suck my cock, I resisted. We had a lot more to do before we got to that stage of the game.

Then again, it could all be part of the game.

"You like that, do you?" I asked, pumping my finger in and out of her mouth, just a little. "I'll bet you'd like it even more if I let you suck my cock."

She whimpered, eyes wide.

"You're probably just dying to reach out and take it in your hands, but you can't, because you're not allowed to move." I pulled my hand away from her and slowly stroked my cock a few times for good measure, watching her watch me.

I stopped only because I was getting too excited myself.

Kneeling between her spread legs, I braced my hands on either side of her and leaned down to kiss her. I let only our lips and tongues touch, keeping my body away from her. She'd want to press up, wrap around me for full-body contact, and I thought I felt her tense to do so before she remembered.

When I was satisfied that she was well-kissed, I moved down to capture one rosy nipple in my mouth. She gasped with pleasure. I suckled gently, teasing her, not giving her the pressure she really wanted. I blew on the wet flesh, watching it pucker. Emily would have loved to thread her hands through my hair and pull my face against her, encouraging me to bite and twist her nipples, but I held off.

Then Emily asked, "Am I allowed to talk?"

I grinned. "Did I say you were gagged?"

"No."

"Then talking's fine."

"I want you to play with my nipples harder," she said.

"What's the magic word?" I trailed my fingertips across her breasts, circling her areolas.

"Please. Oh God, please. I can't stand it!"

I did play with them harder, but gradually, working my way up to nibbling and grazing my teeth against one while I pinched and tweaked the other.

And I stayed there a good long time. I was giving Emily exactly what she wanted, but to the point that it was getting her so aroused that she was going insane. She was reduced to babbling and imploring me to lick her, to touch her clit, to do *something*.

I let her beg for a few minutes, because it was turning me on something fierce, before I left a trail of kisses down her abdomen and turned my attentions to between her spread thighs.

She was so wet, her lips swollen and her clit pouting. I wanted to dive in and lick her, taste her, feel her quiver and hear her scream as I brought her to orgasm again and again.

Instead, I slowly slid one finger into her. Her inner muscles clenched around me, but it wasn't enough to make her come, just drive her a little more crazy.

I removed my finger, caressed her gently from pussy to clit to ass, leaving a glistening trail. I slipped inside her again, gave a little teasing crook of my finger, and pulled out to the sound of her hissed breath.

I used her own moisture as I played with her anus, just around the opening. Then I pulled out my next items: a bottle of lube and a string of anal beads.

Her eyes widened.

Coating my fingers, I carefully slid in and out of her, making sure she was relaxed and comfortable before I slid the beads in, one by excruciating one. I swear the hair on her forearms was standing up by the time I was finished.

I tugged on the string, just a little, as she got used to the feeling of the beads stuffed inside her. I swear her clit was twitching. I'd never seen Emily so aroused, so on edge.

Bondage, even only verbally enforced, was very, very good for her.

Finally I indulged my own desires and bent forward to lick her. I ran my tongue between her lips and all the way around her before flicking lightly against her clit. Her hips twitched, but she kept her butt firmly on the bed, as much as it must have been driving her crazy not to push against the fleeting pressure and find her release.

"You've been very good," I said. "Here's your reward."

I fluttered my tongue against her needy clit and at the same time, as she started to pitch over the edge, I pulled the anal beads from her.

Emily screamed.

Her hands were clenched, her wrists pressed against her thighs as if they were actually trapped there. Her hips rocked up a little, but no more than they would if her ankles were tethered to the bedposts. Her face contorted, her head thrashed back and force, and the muscles in her neck stood out in relief from the force of her orgasm and her efforts not to move with it. Just as I'd imagined when we'd talked a few days ago, her hair was a wild tangle around her, and her body glistened with a light coat of sweat.

Gorgeous. Wild and lustful and just plain gorgeous.

My cock ached from want, and after that performance, I saw no need to hold off.

When I thought she might be able to answer a simple question, I asked her, "Do you want me to come in your pussy or your mouth?"

Emily licked her lips. "My mouth. Please."

She twitched, started to sit up. "Hold still," I said. "I'll let you know when you can move."

I shifted position, lifted her head so I could stick a pillow under it.

Then I more or less knelt down over her face, stuck my cock into her mouth and began moving it in and out—slowly at first, a tease for both of us. "I'm fucking your mouth tonight," I said. "Hold still and suck. I'll do most of the work."

Keeping the patter up was enough tough with her hot little mouth around me, my cock moving between her lips, the slight tug of her teeth now and then. But as I started moving faster and she caught the rhythm, sucking harder, caressing me with tongue and lips and pressure as I pushed in and out, talking coherently became out of the question. I was holding back as best I could, trying not to gag her, making myself resist the urge to fuck her mouth as hard and fast as I would her pussy.

It wasn't easy. I was close, so close. I needed just a little more stimulation.

"Move," I growled. "Use your hands...please..."

One hand fluttered up to play with my taut balls, sending waves of sensation that almost pushed me over the edge.

I couldn't see her dip into her dripping sex, but she must have, because the finger suddenly circling my anus was slick with moisture.

She didn't need to press inside. That did it, that sure, delicate touch.

I lost touch with the planet and pretty much everything on it except my dick for a few delicious seconds as I filled her mouth.

It was all I could do to crawl a little forward so I didn't actually land on her face when I collapsed.

"May I move?" she asked. I nodded—talking was still beyond me.

"Love you," she muttered. "That was...wow." She squirmed so that, lying more or less on her stomach, she could throw one leg and one arm over me.

She may have said something else, but I couldn't be sure because the next thing I knew it was almost dawn and we were still tangled together, her body holding me immobile as my words had held her.

The Brinks Job

My palms were sweating, my hands slick on the steering wheel. I glanced in my rear view mirror. The dark sedan had been following me for several miles, even when I'd turned on Slater and looped around across the park at Kingston to try and shake him.

Nope, he was definitely following me, despite my defensive driving training. Nobody came through this industrial area after hours unless they lived in the development on the other side.

Or they were looking for an illegal rave on a Saturday night.

Or they were planning to hold up a Brinks van, like the one I was driving.

The fact that I knew about the hold-up, knew even the identity of the person in the dark sedan and had planned the heist with him, didn't matter.

He gunned the accelerator. Spraying gravel pinged against my window as he tore out in front of me and wrenched the wheel sideways, effectively cutting me off.

I slammed on the brakes, adrenaline making my ears ring and my vision sharp. I had been trained for this, and my hand automatically went to my gun before I remembered I'd wisely removed all the bullets.

It wasn't just adrenaline coursing through my system, either. My nipples had beaded the moment I'd stepped up into the truck half an hour ago, and I'd been squirming in my seat as I drove, my clit throbbing gently in time with the engine.

My pursuer was at my door, face ominously covered by a black ski mask, gun shoved in the space where I'd cracked the window for air.

Unsure what to do, I put my hands on the steering wheel, in plain sight.

"Get out of the van, Kay."

Hearing my name almost broke me out of the fantasy. But he'd pitched his voice low, gravelly, unfamiliar. I heard the threat, and shivered at the implied danger. If I didn't do what he said…

Reluctantly, I put my hand on the door handle. If I rammed the door open, the gun might go off, and unloaded or not, it was close enough to my head that I didn't want to take the chance. I pulled the lever. It clunked loudly, a sudden counterpoint to my harsh breathing and the drum of blood in my ears.

Donny—I didn't know how else to think of him. My assailant?—took a smooth step back, just far enough so I could open the door.

His gun never wavered. I was impressed, actually.

I eased the door open.

We were both so intent on the moment that neither of us heard the crunch of gravel or the sound of a motor as a second car crept up behind the van.

Police lights flashed, piercing the darkness, half-blinding me. I bit back a scream. Donny threw up an arm to shield his eyes, and I took the advantage. I could have shoved the door open and nailed him with it—but I didn't want to hurt him. Instead, I jumped down from my high perch and grabbed

Donny from behind, my arm around his neck and his arm behind his back before he could fight back.

"Freeze!" the cop shouted. "Put your hands in the air!"

"Well, which is it?" Donny asked. "Do I freeze, or put my hands in the air?"

Dammit. I couldn't stifle a snicker. It didn't help that Marc had his big ol' mirrored cop glasses on in the middle of the night.

"Don't give me any lip, boy," Marc snarled. Metal clinked as he deftly unhooked his handcuffs from his belt.

The cuffs glinted in the strobing light. Despite myself, I shivered, right down to my damp panties.

Let the games begin.

"Nice work, ma'am," Marc said. He was staying in character well, except for the obvious bulge in the crotch of his polyester cop pants. He took Donny from me and slapped one end of the cuffs around Donny's left wrist.

As planned, I ran to the back of my van and unlocked the door. The back was empty, of course. I didn't get to carry money around when I was off duty.

Empty except for a queen-sized mattress and an array of pillows, which in fact made it pretty full. The mattress filled the back from wall to wall and was bent up a bit on one side where a rack attached to the wall interfered with it lying flat. If there had been racks on both walls, we'd have been in trouble.

Marc secured the other cuff to the rack. I knelt on the mattress next to Donny and whispered, "You're doing great, honey. Do you remember your safeword?"

He licked his lips. "Daffodil." His voice was hoarse.

I kissed him, a deep kiss with an interplay of tongue that made me tremble. We'd been together for three years now, and his kisses still held so much promise of things to come.

Oh yeah, we were going to have fun tonight. I put my hand on his thigh, slid it slowly up in search of his...

"I'll take it from here, ma'am," Marc said, returning from turning off his car lights. I noticed that he'd also retrieved a small duffel bag. "It's my job to interrogate the criminals."

I squeezed Donny's hand reassuringly, and retreated to the other side of the van. I loosened my jeans and stretched out comfortably at the other end of the mattress, leaning back against the metal wall. I'd let Marc call the shots now, as we'd planned earlier.

My boyfriend had admitted from the start that he was bi-curious, but had never found the right way to explore his interest. Marc, on the other hand, was unabashedly bi, something I'd learned when I dated him, very briefly, when we were both at the police academy. We later determined that we were far better as friends. We'd stayed close even after I left the force to do private security work, and then he and Donny had become friends as well. The three of us frequently hung out together.

Naturally, our conversation had turned to sex. You might have expected the three of us just to tumble into bed for a sweaty, extended romp punctuated only by ordering pizza, but we all have a flair for the dramatic. Plus, Donny needed an added incentive to push his curiosity into reality. He wasn't submissive per se, but he wanted to let someone else take control, to allow him to feel less responsible for what was happening to him.

What started as a drunken chat after Sunday-football-and-beer had turned into an elaborate scheme involving a local map, schedule coordination, and detailed shopping lists. I swear we synchronized our watches.

It was all turning out wonderfully so far.

The light in the back of the van cast a wavery, anemic glow on both guys. It washed out colors and blurred some details, but I knew them well enough that I could fill in Marc's warm, swarthy complexion and dark eyes, Donny's fairer skin, which would be flushed now with excitement, his sandy hair, now tousled by the ski mask.

When Marc knelt down beside Donny, grabbed handfuls of that sandy hair and pulled him into a brutal kiss, everything snapped into focus for me, despite the poor light.

Donny was on his knees, unable to struggle much even if he'd wanted to due to the way he was cuffed. (Real police cuffs hurt if you struggle. Donny had been coached to stay fairly still until we could get something on him designed for restraining lovers rather than suspects, but we couldn't resist giving him that initial shock of cold metal.) For a second, Donny froze, unsure what to do. His free arm stayed at his side, but I saw it twitching as if he wanted to put it around Marc and pull him even closer.

His body, though—his body knew how to react. He knelt up, rising to give himself more to the kiss. His hips strained forward, pressing against Marc.

I imagined their cocks touching through fabric. It was easy to imagine Donny getting harder, pushing at the fabric of his sweat pants, easy to imagine the heat rising in him. I'd seen it often enough. I'd caused it often enough. But it would be different now, feeling himself brushing against the length and hardness of another man for the first time. While Marc and I hadn't been ideal romantic partners, I certainly had fond memories of his body. I felt a stab of heat imagining how it must seem to Donny. Bigger than it was really was, probably, magnified by imagination, lust and a bit of fear. He'd be thinking about what might happen next, where that cock might end up.

And God knows, I was thinking about that too, and the thought was making me frantic. I slid one hand inside my jeans and stroked gently at my eager clit.

Donny had told me his fantasies, whispered at night in the dark. I'd encouraged him, telling him stories Marc had told me about two men together. Donny had liked some of those an awful lot. After he fell asleep, I scribbled down everything I remembered, and that's what I'd passed on to Marc.

But tonight wasn't only about fulfilling Donny's fantasies. Long before I'd met Marc, I'd masturbated to the idea of being with two hot men. I'm greedy, and more cock to enjoy (not to mention two pairs of arms to wrap around me, two sets of nipples to tease…) sounded like a great plan. Once Marc told me some of his adventures, the fantasies expanded. I wanted to see men together, men kissing, men sucking and fucking, beautiful male bodies doing wonderful, nasty things to each other as well as to me.

And now I was getting my chance.

Donny's arm jerked again, then went around Marc's back, sliding down to his bum. I knew exactly what cop uniform pants felt like, imagined the unappealing texture and under it the far more appealing curve of a fine male ass.

The kissing continued for a long time, enough time for me to decide the jeans and shirt were in my way and scramble out of them. My panties had soaked through already.

It was tempting to make myself come now, but I decided that if I enjoyed the show while teasing myself at a leisurely pace, it would be that much stronger in the end.

Marc broke away from the kiss first and said something I couldn't quite hear, prompting me to crawl closer.

Donny's eyes were wide.

"I said, did you like that?"

Donny didn't answer. I wasn't sure if that was part of the game or if something in his brain had short-circuited.

"Take off your clothes," Marc said, his voice husky and commanding.

"I can't." Donny sounded shaky. I'd almost feel sorry for him except I knew how lust could break up his voice. He took a breath and composed himself. "I really can't. Not hand-cuffed like this."

"Let it be noted that the prisoner refused to cooperate, so we had to step up the interrogation efforts." Marc's smile was deliciously evil. I'd been on the receiving end of that smile before. Usually what happened next made me come a lot. He wasn't hardcore kinky, but he was a master of the fun head-fuck.

As he proved when he reached down to his belt, pulled off a butterfly knife and opened it with a practiced flick.

I'd thought Donny's eyes were wide before.

Marc started at the bottom of the worn black T-shirt and cut up, not a grand slash, but a careful, controlled gesture.

Donny held his breath. I think I did too, because in the silence I could hear the tiny noise of fabric parting.

Marc paused, stretched out the neck opening as wide as it would go, cut at the fabric.

The shirt fell entirely open and Donny let out of an *ooof* of held breath.

Another snick cut the drawstring on Donny's sweats, which tried to fall around his knees but hung up on his erection.

Donny moved his free hand to wriggle the pants down, but Marc beat him to it, brushing along his cock lightly as he got the pants out of the way.

Oh yeah, my guy was enjoying this.

Putting the knife away, Marc rose, one hand following the line of Donny's torso as he did. "Could you give me a hand here, ma'am?" he said, a gleefully ironic tone on the *ma'am*. "Cuff the prisoner's hands in front of him. I have another set of cuffs in the bag."

He tossed me the key for the police cuffs, but before I unlocked those, I rummaged through the duffel. Nestled between a box of condoms and a coil of rope, I found what I was looking for.

Marc might not be hardcore kinky, but he was kinky enough to invest in some sweet toys. The cuffs were thick, cushy, cobalt blue leather, lined with sheepskin for comfort. The straps that actually held them shut were black for contrast. They fastened together with a metal clip.

I fastened one around Donny's free wrist, then reached behind him to unlock the metal cuff that held him to the van wall. He leaned back into me, his body hot against mine.

"Doing all right, love?" I asked. I ran my hands over his hips to cradle his balls as I asked. Parts of him were doing just fine, but I wanted to make sure his brain was as well.

"God, yes." He craned his neck, clearly wanting a kiss, and I was glad to give it to him.

I imagined I could taste Marc on his breath, and that made me want to devour him. The position was awkward, though, so I reluctantly let him go and finished releasing him from the wall.

Finishing the job of re-cuffing him took longer than Marc probably expected, but not because Donny was struggling.

Once I moved in front of him, I had to kiss him again, feeling his arms around me, his warm strength, the urgency of his erection straining to rub against my slickness if he couldn't enter me. Partly it was pure pleasure, both sexual and emotional. Partly, I was feeling a little competitive after watching Donny respond so eagerly to Marc's world-class kissing effort. I was glad to find that he seemed equally eager with me.

Then, once I did get him cuffed, I had to take advantage of his relative helplessness to suckle on his nipples, which always makes him squirm.

Finally, though, I turned him back to Marc and sat back down. The metal wall felt cold against my bare skin, but I figured the action would soon be hot enough to distract me.

Marc had taken advantage of the interruption to undress.

Nice view. Definitely a nice view. I hadn't seen Marc naked in more than six years, but he hadn't let himself go after getting out of the academy, like a lot of cops do. His abs and pecs and thighs were as muscular as they'd been when we were doing intense workouts every morning. *Buff* was the word. Buff and strikingly hairless in certain areas. That was new, but I could see why he did it. His cock, which I remembered as being good-sized, but not gigantic, looked immense and inviting springing straight from his body without a thicket of fur.

I tore my gaze from that pretty sight long enough to glance at Donny.

He wasn't quite drooling, but it was close. Something else seemed to be mixed in with the excitement. Probably nerves. I reached out and put my hand on his arm to reassure him, but he hardly seemed to notice, so taken with the gorgeous hunk of man in front of him.

(This was almost funny, because I knew he'd seen Marc naked a lot more recently than I had, in a gym locker room sort of way. But I suppose with the entire recreational basketball league in there too, he hadn't ventured to take a good long look.)

Time seemed to stop in the back of the van. None of us moved. I don't think we even breathed. In the distance, the sound of a siren cut through even the armored walls of the van. I went even more still, thinking some good citizen taking a shortcut might have phoned in what looked like a Brinks van in trouble, before I correctly identified the sound.

"Ambulance, not police," Marc breathed what I'd just processed.

Having to speak broke the spell. Marc stepped forward, gave Donny a gentle shove that didn't so much push him backward as signal him to lie down. Without being directed, he put his bound hands above his head, giving Marc free access to his body.

I hadn't been sure what would actually happen once the guys got naked together. Given the scenario, I'd imagined a little rough stuff, Marc using a bit of force to pretend-take what Donny wanted to give anyway. That was one of his fantasies, but it was one of many.

Instead, Marc lay down on top of him and started another of those incredible kisses.

There's only so much a girl can take. I lay down with them at a skewed angle so I could, with a little effort, see both faces and Marc's glorious butt. Then I began to kiss and stroke wherever I could reach on either of them.

Even through the muffling kiss, Donny was making low, animal noises. The van was starting to smell like male musk, accented by my own arousal.

Marc raised his head and began kissing his way down Donny's body. He lingered at one nipple, the one further from me.

Again, what's a girl to do? If one mouth on one nipple would make Donny ecstatic, two ought to do better.

Apparently it did, if the indrawn breath and the squirming were to be believed.

When Donny was bucking and wriggling, Marc shifted again and continued kissing his way down my boy's torso. I kept working on the nipples and enjoying the view.

Marc licked and kissed down, breathed on the rampant dick without actually touching it and kissed his way to the hipbone, where he rested his cheek.

I knew that move: letting the anticipation build for both of you, drinking in the intimate, animal scent of your lover's balls. I don't think I've ever been able to keep it up for long, though. Marc couldn't either.

I held my breath as his hand closed around the base of Donny's cock.

Donny groaned, struggled against the cuffs.

Marc's mouth opened. Before he filled it, though, he looked at me. "Get on his face or something, Kay. Not much point in having a threesome if everyone's not getting some."

The sound coming out of Donny was inarticulate enough that he had to repeat it before we understood. "Daffodil."

We froze. "You all right? Do you need to stop?" Marc asked, moving his hand.

"Please. Don't stop. Don't move...your hand away. It's wonderful." The words sounded like words again, but he was pausing between them like a graduate of the William Shatner School of Acting. "But the cuffs. I want...if Kay...I want to...

touch you both."

Marc grinned. "Kay, honey, I think our criminal's done his time. Let him loose and see if he attacks us."

"We can only hope!"

After I unfastened Donny's wrists, I considered straddling his face, then reconsidered. This was his first time ever with a man. He should get to enjoy all the aspects, including visual. Instead, I cuddled up next to him, took his hand, and put it where I needed it, right on my throbbing clit.

As Marc's mouth closed on his cock, Donny rolled over and bit my shoulder. So much for my generosity in letting him see.

"Is it good?" I asked—a silly question under the circumstances, but dirty talk is dirty talk, and Donny liked it. "Does it feel different, knowing you're being sucked by a man? How do you like Marc's mouth on you?" I wasn't expecting a sensible answer, which was good because I didn't get one. "Your cock looks so beautiful going in and out of his mouth." That got him to look again, and to nod tightly in agreement. "He looks like he's really good at sucking cock. I guess he should be; I know he loves doing it." I couldn't be sure, but I thought I saw Marc flush.

Marc did look like he was good at it, taking Donny in avidly, with a combination of tenderness and speed that was eliciting some pretty extraordinary noises. Despite the distraction, Donny was doing a fine job on me, his fingers circling my clit for a sweet, slow build that gathered in my pelvis waiting for release. But watching the guys was at least as exciting as those sensations. I could never see Donny's face well when I was blowing him; it was quite a study. Did he make those hot, half-pained faces when I was doing it?

And what exactly *was* Marc doing anyway? I felt as though I should be taking notes. Surely I could learn something about sucking cock from someone who had a cock of his own.

He interrupted himself, keeping one hand on Donny's cock but reaching around to fumble in the duffel bag.

He came out with lube, poured some of the thick substance onto his hand and stroked it rather showily down his fingers until they glistened.

"Open up for me," Marc breathed, and moved the lubed hand out of sight. I didn't need X-ray vision to imagine what he was doing, gently but inexorably pushing one finger—maybe the first of several—into my boyfriend's body.

Donny's body tensed.

"Relax," I whispered. "You've done this before. More than this." We'd played with butt plugs sometimes. I hadn't been crazy about the sensation, but Donny had been. "You'll love it. You know you will."

I kissed him and could almost feel the tension draining from him.

Then Marc must have found the sweet spot.

Donny's face flushed clear down to his nipples. His body strained.

"Oh no, not yet." Marc took his mouth away, but left his hands where they were, one working the cock, the other hidden, but obviously playing with Donny's ass. "One more finger at least. And maybe later my cock, unless you suck me off instead." His tone was calm, conversational, but his face wasn't.

The noises Donny was making were barely human.

And when Marc took him in his mouth again, they ceased to be human at all.

I thought that, lost in his own pleasure, Donny had forgotten about me. (I didn't blame him. With all that happening to me, I know I'd lose coordination.) I was just about to take matters into my own hands, relieve the pent-up pressure, when he managed to choke out, "Let me lick you."

I climbed onto his face in record time.

He was moving under me as well as licking, writhing from Marc's attentions and channeling what might have been screams, otherwise, into me. Already on edge from all the voyeuristic fun, I teetered there for a little while, loving his hot mouth, loving the waves of sensation, loving the glorious sight of a handsome naked man pleasuring the man who was pleasuring me.

Donny was shaking. I could see his abs ripple.

And then he bucked his hips. I couldn't see his orgasm, but I could feel it coursing through him, and I could see Marc's eyes light up as Donny's come flooded his mouth.

Those things, more than anything Donny was capable of doing at that moment, pushed me over the edge I'd been teetering on.

It's a good thing Brinks trucks are armored, or they'd have heard me at the housing development five blocks away.

We collapsed in a spent heap on the mattress. A corner of the duffle dug into my hip, but at first I didn't have the energy to reach down to move it. I rested my head on Donny's chest and felt his heartbeat pound against my cheek and listened to the sound of the three of us panting.

Finally I roused myself, threw on my shirt (just long enough to skim the tops of my thighs), and eased out of the back of the truck to retrieve bottles of water out of the cooler in the front seat.

The night air was soft and refreshing, and a few dim lights glowed at the corners of warehouses, not strong enough to dim the sharp glitter of stars above. I paused just long enough to smile up at them, tossing out a silent thanks to anyone who might be listening for the fact that everything was going so well.

When I returned, the tiny space was filled with the hot heady scent of sex and sweat, so strong it made me flutter, deep inside. Donny lay with his head in Marc's lap, eyes half-lidded, stroking Marc's hard cock with languid movements.

Such a sweet picture—except it reminded me that Marc hadn't come yet.

I tossed each of them a water bottle and was rewarded with promises of undying affection. I had to admit it tasted like nectar to me, too. I'd gotten pretty sweaty and dry-mouthed from howling in pleasure.

"What about you, sweetheart?" I asked Marc, joining Donny's hand in its slow caress along the length of Marc's penis. The taut skin was hot, sticky with pre-come. I ran my thumb along the head. Marc's response degenerated into a moan.

Donny took a deep breath. I recognized his expression: He was steeling himself to say something. Was everything okay?

Then he said, "I want...Marc...to fuck me up the ass."

The last words came out in a rush. Oh, my sweet boy!

Marc's cock twitched under our hands.

It only took a moment to change positions on the mattress: Donny on his hands and knees, with Marc crouched behind him. As Marc lubed up his fingers again to prepare Donny's ass for something larger and longer, I scooted beneath Donny and reached for his penis, already half-hard again.

I could taste Marc on him, and Donny's own come, as he grew in my mouth. It didn't take long for him to get fully erect, what with Marc's ministrations, or for Marc to get Donny opened up and relaxed.

Another shift, and I was kneeling in front of Donny. He slid in, and I groaned at the feel of him filling me. Oral sex is all well and good and fun, but there was something about a steely cock buried in me that made my toes curl.

But I had to wait for the actual fucking part, as Marc slowly pressed himself into Donny's virgin ass. I could feel them gently rocking back and forth as Donny opened up enough to let the tip pop in. They both froze for a moment, reveling in the sensation.

Then Marc slowly, relentlessly, slid full length into Donny. I know because it made Donny press deeper into me.

It was awkward at first, setting up a rhythm that we all moved to. It wasn't perfect—we had moments of rueful laughter as things went awry at times—but it was *right*. Donny whimpered my name, then Marc's. I could only guess what he was feeling. I just knew it had to be exquisite.

Knowing what they were doing set off a chain of hot images in my head, pushing me on. I imagined I could feel Marc's cock inside Donny's, both of them stretching me, filling me, fucking me.

Donny reached around me, cupping my breast, pinching my nipple. Then I felt another hand rub my ass—the same side—and realized Marc was reaching around to touch me, too. We didn't exactly form a circle, but at the same time it was much more than a simple line. We were all touching each other, all connected by energy and arousal…and love.

That last bit didn't penetrate my lust-fogged brain clearly. It was just part of all of the images and sensations and intensity. I felt it more than I thought it.

It was a combination of everything that sent me over the edge: the emotions, and the feeling of a hard cock in me, and the vision of how Donny and Marc looked together on repeated loop in my mind's eye. I was screaming again, and the boys were joining me. I felt Donny's cock swell inside me just before he shot his load, and his frantic pumping was matched by Marc's. Yes, oh yes, oh…

We collapsed in a heap again, somehow ending up with me in the center, cuddled close by both boys, who clasped hands together across my stomach.

We couldn't stay this way for long. I had to have the truck back well before dawn, before anyone noticed its absence, and we'd have to clean out the back thoroughly before that. (Marc had used his own car, with the detachable police light on the dash.) But I wasn't ready to move quite yet.

I felt safe. Warm. Loved.

I loved Donny, and he loved me. I hadn't been able to commit to Marc as a solo relationship, but now, now I wondered… Could the three of us…?

It was too soon to say. And if we just all stayed as good friends, that would be fine, too.

Either way, it had been a hell of a ride.

Sacred Places

The drizzle of gray rain had driven the other tourists away from the monastery ruins growing out of the rugged Welsh landscape.

Kathleen stared at the altar—at what had once been an altar, but was now desecrated stone, robbed of its relics and smashed in half by Henry VIII's men centuries ago.

The words at the information plaque were a meaningless blur. So desolate here. Did anyone truly know what went on, day after day, night after night, if no outsiders were visiting?

She swore she could hear the monks chanting, low and melodious. Was the Latin in praise to God or some darker ritual?

A little ways away, Ted picked his way through the shin-high ruined walls that delineated the monks' tiny cells. His scarlet rain slicker hood was up, his head down. The monks would all have been in brown or white, no way to distinguish one from the other when their hoods obscured their faces. Even harder when it was dark, the only light from a flickering lamp or candle that tossed shadows across their mysterious features.

She'd never admitted it to anyone—not to former lovers, not to Ted, barely even to herself. There was kinky, and there was *kinky*, and for a former Catholic like herself, this was beyond even that.

Was that why she'd suggested they turn off here to see the ruined monastery in the Welsh mountains? It wasn't on their itinerary, but when she'd caught sight of the signpost, she'd blurted out the request.

To indulge her deepest, darkest fantasy? Or to receive penance for it?

And that was when the full-on shudder hit her, arousal clenching at her sex, her nipples and clit suddenly, almost painfully sensitive.

"Are you okay?" Ted had come up beside her. "You're cold; we should go."

"No, I'm fine," she said, and her voice betrayed her, a husky tremble that Ted had to recognize.

Either that, or the flush she knew had crept around her neck, and maybe the glassy look that had to be in her eyes.

"Kath?"

"I'm hearing voices," she managed. "Music."

He pointed to the side of the plaque on the wall of what had been the chapel, and she saw the little speaker grill. "They've got some Gregorian chant piped in. Pretty impressive when they don't even have a visitor's center."

She laughed nervously. "Of course." Of course she wasn't hallucinating. Of course Ted was the least monk-like creature she could imagine…yet in her current state of mind, she could envision his blue eyes brilliant and just barely visible under a woolen hood, his powerful body hinted at but not entirely disguised by his robe… Although he'd have to lose his thick, shoulder-length dark hair, which would be a shame.

Bending close, he whispered in her ear, "I know that look. Kathleen Brigid Murphy, were you having dirty thoughts about monks?" He sounded stern, but she recognized unholy erotic glee when she heard it. The combination slew her every time.

Her cheeks flamed far more than she could blame on the spring breeze—and her cunt twitched, as hot as her face and, she realized, growing as wet as the mist on the breeze.

"No…" The denial was instinct. Some fantasies were just too weird, too shameful to confess, even to a husband who seemed utterly unshockable (and had a few weird fantasies of his own).

On the other hand, the remnants of Catholic guilt insisted honesty was the best policy, and so far it had been where Ted and sex were concerned. Every time she'd confessed a sexual fantasy, he'd gotten hard and hot and bothered and had done his best to enact it—usually with mindblowing results.

"Okay, yes. I was thinking dirty things about monks. You happy now?" Merely whispering the words made her stomach lurch with a combination of nerves and arousal, made her breath come faster, made her lace bra feel stiff and scratchy against her insistent nipples.

"Tell me more."

She glanced around. The sun was starting to push through the streaked clouds, and any minute now a vanload of senior citizens could descend on the chapel ruins. Kathleen had lost a lot of her shyness since getting involved with Ted, but complete strangers, especially the elderly ones she imagined, didn't need to overhear her darker fantasies. "Later. Back at the B&B."

She should've known better than to try and negotiate. It always made things worse for her in the end.

So why was she suddenly wetter?

Ted smiled an evil smile full of dangerous promises. "Oh no. You're telling me now. Right here." He backed her up into the chapel until her trembling thighs hit the ruined altar and she was forced to half-sit on the broken stones.

She went unresisting. Wouldn't have been able to resist if she'd wanted to, and she didn't. When Ted decided to be all dominant and alpha like that, she turned to putty—and the fact she'd been mentally tied to an altar and waiting to be ravished by anonymous monks made the puttying process that much faster.

He close against her, thigh to thigh, and slid his hands down her arms. His grip was loose, but he pinned her arms to her sides as effectively as if he'd used leather straps.

"Tell me," he repeated, and she knew better than to disobey a second time.

She told him how she felt the cold stone against her back, her ass, her legs. How coarse hemp rope—the rope of monks' belts—abraded her wrists and ankles where she was bound. She could smell beeswax and burning from the countless candles surrounding her, and myrrh and frankincense heavy in the air.

The candle wax, she knew, would be put to good use soon. She stifled a moan.

She was naked in the dark stone chapel, but that wasn't why she shivered. Fear and arousal mixed, a perfect, heady blend, and moisture was pooling between her spread-eagled thighs. At first, all she could hear was pigeons among the high, vaulted arches, cooing and rustling their wings. Then, distantly, came chanting, a solemn sound growing louder, and she shuddered right down to her clit.

Now the monks filed in, two by two in procession. Their chant didn't sound like any hymn she'd ever heard—pious, but laden with erotic promise. They were robed, hooded, anonymous, their faces lost in flickering shadow.

They surrounded her. Hands reached out…

Kathleen struggled for air, unable to keep talking. If Ted hadn't been standing so close, she thought she would have swayed and fallen.

"Well, well," Ted said, his low breath hot against her ear as he held her. "You do have a vivid little fantasy there, don't you? Tell me, do they pinch your nipples hard, like you like it? Do they drip wax on them? Do they reach between your thighs and tease your clit, laughing at how wet you are, at how close you get to coming before they pull away, denying you your release? Do they untie you and drape you face first over the altar and whip your tender ass with birch branches, telling you how wicked you've been and how you need to be punished for your sins?"

His dirty litany not only built on her profane and secret confessions—it delved into her psyche and brought to light erotic details even she hadn't admitted to herself. The pressure had been growing inside her since they arrived. Now, with his obviously hard cock pressing against her sex and her mind racing with visions that aroused and shamed her in equal measure, she couldn't hold back.

And Ted knew it.

"Show the monks what a slut you are," he said, and she exploded, grinding against him even as she buried her face in his shoulder to muffle her screams.

When she stopped shaking, she grabbed his arm, tugging him back toward the rental car.

Ted tugged back, holding her in place. "Where do you think you're going?"

"Back to the car. I want to get to you someplace more private."

Three older women with binoculars were heading up from the parking lot and Kathleen's still hungry body thought it was past time to get to the B&B and finish what they'd started.

"Not so fast. We haven't seen everything yet."

That was a change. She was usually the one saying that to Ted, who wasn't as fascinated with ruins as she was. And he never, ever put off a chance to have sex.

Unless, she realized with a sudden tug in her cunt, putting it off might make things more interesting later.

He put his hand on the back of her neck. His voice dropped to a throaty whisper that seemed to caress her clit as he said, "Take all the time you'd like here. I want you to have plenty of time to drink in the atmosphere and think about monks and the wickedness of your ways. A girl like you could ruin an entire monastery."

His voice, and the images it brought to mind of hooded figures and anonymous hands and vows of celibacy being thrown away like the day's trash, were enough to push Kathleen back to the trembling edge of orgasm.

*

Even without the sacrilegious pleasure of her fantasy, the monastery was worth closer exploration. As the sun came out, it became easier to imagine it intact, with robed brothers working in the herb garden, praying in the chapel, going about their day. At the same time, the contrast between bright sun and dark shadows made the ruins seem all that much more lonely and haunted, especially in the chapel, where the walls were just intact enough to give the feeling of a building instead of rubble in the general outline of buildings. It was easy to imagine the chapel filling with ghostly monks at night—and who knew what depravities ghostly monks might practice?

The longer she spent there, the harder it was separate herself from the fantasy.

And the few miles from the monastery to the B&B seemed like a trek across Asia.

*

They celebrated their arrival at the B&B with a round of fucking that made Kathleen fear for the antique bed—at least until she reached a point where she didn't give a damn about the bed anymore. It was hard, athletic, straightforward sex, with little connection to deviant monks, other than a few teasing sentences that got lost in the pursuit of more immediate pleasures, but Kathleen couldn't complain. Sharing the fantasy led to hot sex, and after all, that was what fantasies were for— even the ones that left you flushed and trembling with shame.

Ted was still flashing back to the interlude at the monastery himself, though, judging from some of the heated looks he gave her while they checked out the 11th-century church in the town center, or the way he insisted they have a drink in The Tipsy Friar pub.

If Ted was still thinking about it, that meant it might crop up in some creative way when she least expected it. Would he enact some element of it, or perhaps put her through "confession" and "penance" for having evil fantasies about holy men? Would he have her on her knees in front of him, admitting her wickedness in explicit detail? Torture her sins out of her like an inquisitor?

She shuddered with exquisite fear over her cider.

Unfortunately the cider conspired with several previous nights of more sex than sleep, and soon Kathleen was yawning over the last inch or so of her pint. "I need a nap," she confessed, taking her glasses off and rubbing her eyes. "Want to curl up with me?"

"I'll walk you back and tuck you in, but I need to pick up a few supplies in the shops."

She assumed he meant razors or deodorant, but by the time he returned with several shopping bags, she'd been asleep for a couple of hours and it was getting dark. He wasn't that into retail therapy, even in a place with a lot more shopping options than this town. Which meant he was up to something…but what?

From the secrecy and the smile, it had to be something erotic and exciting. And she was willing to bet that it had something to do with the taboo scene they'd woven in the monastery ruins. But what?

The conviction became a sexy certainty when he told her to wear a skirt and no panties to the country inn where they had dinner reservations. But nothing happened during dinner beside the usual flirting.

Comfortably full of venison pâté and salmon, pleasantly relaxed from Pinot Noir, lulled by Ted's hand on her knee, Kathleen took a few minutes to realize that Ted was driving further out of town instead of back to the B&B.

"Where are we going?" she asked, although she had a wet, slippery, nervously excited feeling that she knew.

"Back to the monastery. It's past Compline on the Feast of Saint Bacchus and the good brothers are waiting for you."

He turned on the CD player and Gregorian chant poured out, spooky and stark and curiously sensual.

Arousal slammed into her like a fist. As they drove through the dark countryside, *Kyrie Eleison* soared around them. Ted's face was remote and he refused to answer her questions, saying all would be revealed in good time and then falling into silence so profound he might have been a holy statue on an altar—except for his fingers stroking the soft flesh of her inner thigh and occasionally teasing her labia and dip into her cunt before retreating. By the time they arrived at the monastery she was moaning and keening through bitten lips, wanting to beg to come yet, perversely, not wanting the erotic torment to end.

Curious and yet terrified to discover what her devious husband had laid in store for her.

The monastery ruins seemed deserted, not a car in the parking lot, not a sound other than the small bird-and-insect noises of night in the country.

But she could see candles burning in the chapel, just a few lights dancing in the darkness.

Kathleen's heart was pounding so hard she could hardly breathe, and her juices ran down her suddenly shaky thighs.

What had Ted done? He'd been with her for the past few hours. Would candles stay lit that long?

He couldn't have gotten other people in on this. Or could he?

She laughed with relief (or disappointment? she didn't want to consider that) when they got into the chapel area and she saw no one else there.

The candles were the battery-operated kind and somehow—she couldn't begin to fathom how—Ted had procured a folding table, which he'd set up over the altar ruins and covered with a tarp. It was sweet, but it was kind of cheesy and…

Then he lifted his oversized sweatshirt and she saw the coarse rope he'd wrapped around his waist—the rope he was now unwinding with the obvious intent of binding her down—and something inside her broke. She no longer saw battery-operated candles or a modern folding table or even the stars twinkling between the empty flying buttresses.

Instead she saw an arched ceiling half-lost in darkness and an altar draped with a richly embroidered purple cloth. She believed the candles were real and the melted wax painfully hot.

And she had no will to resist when Ted led her to the table and helped her onto it, when he bound her ankles and wrists (dimly she knew the knots were loose, for quick escape if someone arrived, but she somehow really believed she was firmly tied down and utterly, completely, erotically helpless).

Gently, he took her glasses off and tucked them safely away, then draped a cloth over her eyes. Not a full mask, but something with a loose weave.

"Can't have you seeing their faces," Ted said, his voice low. "Can't have you telling. This way, you'll just have to guess how many there are. How many touching you. How many watching as you writhe and plead and come again and again."

Oh, dear God, he was right. Through the gauzy material she could see the flickering candlelight, which cast shadows—shadows that could be just shadows or could be robed men, moving closer to stand in a ring around her, gazing at her half-naked, spread-eagled, vulnerable form.

Then she heard a crinkle followed by a striking match, and smelled beeswax, and her gut clenched and if she could have squeezed her thighs together she would have come right then.

He'd already hiked her skirt up around her hips. Now he unbuttoned her blouse and the front snap of her bra. Her already aching nipples crinkled harder in the cool night air.

"Wicked girl," Ted said hoarsely. He tweaked both of her nipples, twisting them to the point of glorious pain. She arched her hips helplessly. "Fantasizing about men of the cloth. Dreaming of them doing unspeakable things to you, all in the name of earthly pleasures, pleasures of the flesh. Believing your perverse sexual desires are sacred."

He released her throbbing nipples then, snaking a hand down between her thighs. As he had in the car, he toyed with her almost languidly, his fingers skidding through her wetness, but without enough pressure to bring her to the release she so desperately craved.

"Please," she managed. "Please."

"You have the audacity to beg?" he said. Whether the deep voice was Ted or an anonymous monk, she didn't know. Didn't care. The hazy covering over her eyes meant she could imagine it both ways.

Then, without warning, the first drop of wax hit her already tender nipple. The heat spread from her breast to her cunt, turning her body to molten lava. More searing wax, and she came, hard, muffling her own screams out of shame and fear, her shuddering body rattling the table beneath her.

Ted didn't let her rest or enjoy any after-orgasm languor. Before the final aftershocks had died away, he was already untying her, hauling her to her unsteady feet and turning her around, only to bind her face down shortways across the table.

She didn't know if she should be relieved that he hadn't managed to find a birch branch, but really, his broad hand on her naked ass was enough. He moved around her, smacking her with different hands and making it seem that the blows were coming from multiple men all around her. The shamed, excited part of her rode that feeling, believed the shadows conjured by her blurred vision until she could almost convince herself she could hear their voices, feel their woolen robes brushing her bare skin. The slaps were gunshots in the still night air, gunshots that ricocheted through her pussy, bringing her closer to the edge.

Ted (a monk?) moved around the table and faced her.

She actually worked one hand free so she could wrap her fingers around him, adding her hand to the ministrations of her mouth.

She was so close, almost desperate, but she knew she couldn't come like this, with her thighs spread wide and nothing touching her clit or driving into her. And the fact that her whole body screamed for release when the only release in sight was Ted's seemed perversely perfect.

Because there was more, more that she'd whispered to Ted in their B&B, her face flushed with shame and arousal. The monks tied her down and whipped her for having unholy sexual thoughts, for not being chaste. But when they saw how aroused she was—saw the wetness slicking her inner thighs, saw her hard, pouting nipples, saw her body arching and begging—then *they* succumbed to lust. The sight of her willing, wanton body was too much for them.

Because of *her*, they chose earthly pleasures—sexual release—over God Himself.

The thought of the monks coming for her and her alone, of them crying out God's name when they were really spurting their seed for her, on her, in her, was the crux of her fantasy.

Ted's hips jerked in a short, staccato rhythm, and she knew he was there. She tasted his first spurt on her tongue, and then he pulled back and splashed his come on her face, twitching and groaning.

She couldn't come like this, and yet she did, her cunt spasming as her orgasm wrenched through her, twisting her and releasing her.

This time she did scream, taking God's name in vain over and over again. Ted's cries joined with hers.

And as the echoes died away, they were together, at one with each other and with their private deity.

Drastic Measures

The piano teacher didn't look at all like what Paul had expected.

When he'd enquired at the local music store, the woman there said, "Oh, Stella's the best there is. She's been teaching for years."

And at his regular Sunday dinner at his brother's house in Lexington, outside of Boston, his nephew Jack had referred to her as "Old Ms. Keach." His lessons hadn't lasted long. "She expected me to *practice*," he'd said with all the disdain that a twelve-year-old boy could muster, which was surprisingly a lot.

So when Paul pulled up outside the two-story 1940s cottage with white shutters, bordered by a colorful riot of autumn flowers, he had a mental picture of Ms. Keach pretty solidly in his head.

The woman who answered the door *was*, he realized, "old" to a twelve-year-old. He pegged her in her early 50s, about ten years older than himself, but she was one of those women who settled into her looks at that age, comfortable and striking. Her hair was the shade of reddish-gold that could almost, but not quite, be called strawberry blond, and it was piled messily into a topknot on her head. She wore flat sandals and a flowered dress of some floaty material that skimmed just below her knees.

For a confused moment he thought she might be someone else who lived in the house, but then she smiled, and he saw the lines around her eyes and mouth. On her, they fit.

"Paul Nabholz?" she said. "I'm Stella Keach. You're punctual. Good. That's a requirement."

They shook hands; her fingers were slender but her grip was firm. He supposed that came from years of playing piano.

"My studio's out back," she said. "Follow me."

He followed her along the flower-lined, herringbone-patterned brick path around the right side of the house.

She wasn't his type at all, and yet…and yet he found himself attracted to her, and he wasn't quite sure why. He liked tall women, dark hair, commanding, not pale and floral and floaty. Yet he felt himself get aroused looking at her, smelling that floral perfume, light but not cloying.

A moderate heel would almost bring her to his height, so she wasn't exactly short. And she had a strength to her. Not just in her hands: he saw it in the curve of her pale, freckled triceps beneath the cap sleeves of her dress and in the flexing of her calves as she walked.

"It's quieter here," she explained as she opened the French doors to the small, single-story studio. Although the houses on either side of her were a little close, her backyard was deep, ending in woods, and the studio was tucked in just at the tree line. "Not everybody wants to hear new trombone players or…other noises."

The studio was flooded with light from windows on three sides, although heavy drapes along the sides could be pulled across them if the angle of the sun was too acute.

Stella sat on the piano bench facing away from the piano. Her posture was impeccable, her back ramrod straight even though she looked relaxed. She indicated a wooden stool, the kind that spun, and he sat, feeling a little self-conscious.

"So," she said. "Tell me about yourself and why you want to take piano lessons."

"Well, it's complicated." Not a great start, but it was what it was. "Earlier this year I was in a serious motorcycle accident…" He flexed his fingers, feeling the pull in the back of his right hand from the tendon that had snapped and been stitched back together.

She saw the motion, took his hand in hers, examined the scars, the flattened spot where a now-shattered knuckle had been. Her fingers were gentle but firm.

Her touch felt different than of any of the scores of people who had worked on his hand.

No. His reaction was different. Physical. Visceral.

He barely had time to register that before she released him, and then he felt a surge of almost panic when she said, "I'm not a rehab therapist, Mr. Nabholz. Piano would be good exercise for your hand, but that's not why I teach. I can recommend several other good teachers in the area." She started to stand.

"No, it's not that—there's more to it than that." Dammit, he was going to fuck this up before he even got started. And he didn't know why it suddenly mattered so damn much.

She sat back, one eyebrow raised. "Go on."

"I nearly died," he said. It wasn't something he admitted often, certainly not to strangers, but he got the sense she would accept nothing less than complete honesty. "I was fortunate to get a large settlement, and between that and some good investments, I've been able to take the opportunity to grab life by the horns, so to speak. I've always wanted to play piano. Well, not when I was a kid. My parents suggested I try it, but I was more interested in sports at the time, and then girls. I always regretted that—well, I didn't regret the girls, but by the time I realized chicks dig musicians, it was too late."

She was smiling, the lines around her blue-green eyes and mouth crinkling. "It's never too late, Mr. Nabholz."

"Call me Paul, please. And I don't mean to make light of this. I'm serious about wanting to learn."

"Paul. All right. While I expect you to practice, and be prepared for lessons, if anything I ask you to do causes you undue pain, you will tell me. I will not have you damaging yourself. Is that clear?"

"Yes." Although pain wasn't something he shied away from.

Oh, he knew what she meant: there was a difference between good pain, like muscle soreness after a good work-out, and bad pain, like the kind he'd felt when he'd first woken up in the hospital. It would be flat-out stupid to set back his hand therapy.

But there was another kind of pain, the kind that skimmed the deliciously fine line with pleasure.

That kind, he craved.

Not the pain, exactly, but submitting to the person who had the perfect combination of strength and tenderness to cause it.

He didn't add that the reason he had time on his hands was in part because he'd come home from the hospital to an empty house. His girlfriend, Ashley, had used the accident as an excuse, but in truth, their relationship had frayed almost to the breaking point before that. She hadn't been interested in the level of control he craved to give to her. She'd made an attempt, but her heart hadn't been in it, and he couldn't fault her for not sharing his kink.

"I don't give lessons to many adults," Stella went on. "Most don't have the time or desire to put in the work. Let me be clear: I don't tolerate laziness. If you don't put in the effort, then you're wasting my time. But I think you have the desire, and you obviously are taking the time. Do Tuesdays at 2 p.m. work for you? Evenings and weekends are taken up with school-aged students, I'm afraid."

"Yes, that's fine. Not a problem." Paul felt a warm rush of relief, almost a little delight that he'd passed muster. So far, anyway.

"Wonderful." She stood, picked up a folder from the top of the piano, and held it out to him.

He took it, but his face must have registered confusion, because she smiled again. "Your homework," she said. "It'll let me know where you are in your musical education, and a few other things so I can tailor the lessons to your needs."

*

The paperwork turned out to be a questionnaire, ranging from questions about how well he could read music to what types of music he preferred, and why. He was also tasked with listening to some specific pieces of music and detailing how he felt about them: what he heard, how it made him feel, what he liked or disliked about it. The works ranged from classical to jazz to rock, some he was already familiar with, some he'd never heard before.

Paul put thought and effort into his responses.

Both because he did love music and wanted to understand it better, and because he wanted to make Stella proud.

At first he chalked the desire for her approval up to his general nature. She was a woman in a position of relative authority over him, so it made sense that he'd seek her praise.

Sophie Mouette

At first, he didn't dare dream she'd have the same proclivities as he did, and want to share them with him.

Even if she didn't, the experience was broadening his understanding of domination and submission and his own desires. He'd watched and read erotica and been to clubs and other events in the Boston area, and was used to the trappings of BDSM: the black leather, the spikey high heels, the crops, the dungeons motifs. All that had automatically become part of the fantasy.

But the few times he'd been to clubs, and certainly at the big fetish conferences, he'd admittedly seen people of all shapes and sizes, not just statuesque women wearing perfect corsets and sporting bloodred lips and heavy eye makeup.

It just took him awhile to realize *none* of the trappings were necessary.

It was about attitude, and confidence, and the energy a person exuded.

Stella might be all pale and floral and floaty, but she had a steel core, she knew was she expected of him as a student, and she was entirely in control.

It was so hot, it took his breath away.

He didn't dream, but he could fantasize, and fantasizing about her almost became a requirement, because if he didn't masturbate before his lessons with her, he'd be rock hard the entire time.

*

Paul practiced every day. Well, almost every day. Today had been an exception. He'd been too distracted, and trying to convince himself he needed to practice to please Stella made the hum of arousal and anticipation worse.

A well-known domme from San Francisco, the one who'd literally written the book (well at least *a* book) about female-dominant/male-submissive power exchange, was giving a series of classes for the New England Leather Association.

And by sheer luck of the draw, he was going to be one of her demo bottoms.

Attendees were gathering around black-and-blue-draped folding tables laden with simple hors d'oeuvres and non-alcoholic drinks when he arrived at the class site, an "alternative event space" carved out of a former factory in Chelsea, just outside of Boston. The room—rough brick walls hung with bright paintings by local artists, a scuffed wooden floor still marked by the machines that had stood there in the early twentieth century, floor-to-ceiling windows that looked out toward the lights of the city, and rows of folding chairs that were largely ignored at the moment in favor of socializing and the food table—buzzed with activity. It didn't feel crowded, thanks to its size and high ceiling, but there were forty or so people there and it was early enough more people were bound to filter in. Usually these events attracted a smaller group, but the well-known presenter must have pulled kinksters out of the woodwork—or at least from all over New England. He was definitely seeing faces he hadn't spotted since the big Fetish Flea.

For a second, he hesitated in the doorway. This was his first time playing demo bottom and the larger-than-expected audience was intimidating.

But being intimidated, pleasantly scared, was part of the fun, wasn't it? He sucked in a deep breath, and the familiar scents of coffee and old dust and something else—ancient machine oil, maybe?—that always lingered in the space reminded him he was among his tribe, even if he didn't know everyone here. Then he stepped in and was immediately accosted by several friends and a woman who'd been an occasional play partner, who chatted with him until he was whisked away by one of the organizers to meet with the visiting domme in a "side room" marked off by several folding screens decorated with vintage fetish pictures, with a whip-wielding Bettie Page front and center.

Mistress Marlene—"but you can call me Marl when we're not in a scene"—was small and round, with warm, medium-brown skin, dark eyes, and short-cropped hair dyed a vibrant fire-engine red. Her ready smile and warm expression did nothing to undercut a subtle air of authority and competence. Nothing overt. Nothing pushy. In fact, she came off as friendly yet professional as she explained what she'd be doing, what he might expect, and what he needed to do to be a good demo bottom. But he sensed that if she wanted to exert her will in a more blatantly erotic way, it would be irresistible and a hell of a lot of fun.

Reminded him of Stella.

Which made his already excitable cock twitch and his mouth go dry. Because while he could think of few things hotter than being in this woman's hands for a little while, most of the ones he could think of involved Stella and something with a little more emotional weight to it than being the literal whipping boy as Mistress Marlene demonstrated "head-fucks with singletails" while he was partly clothed and a bunch of people took notes.

Impersonal demo or not, still wearing running shorts or not, Paul was already starting to get into the zone when Mistress Marlene led him into the main room. Yeah, people out there, now sitting in the chairs, but he wasn't focused on them. He was focused on *her*. Couldn't help it. Without a steady lover, he'd learned to enjoy what he could, when he could.

As soon as he heard the first sharp crack of the singletail, nowhere near his skin but still seeming to cut and caress, Paul started to drop. He couldn't, afterward, have explained exactly what happened except that everything was simultaneously frightening and wonderful and nothing truly hurt. A few sharp stings that faded quickly, but most of it was, as promised, head-fucks, playing on the *idea* of a potentially dangerous whip, the noises it made, and the domme's own attitude.

When the demo was finished, Mistress Marlene—Marl again—handed him a bottle of water and an oatmeal-raisin cookie. A couple of his friends from the community converged on him, one with a fuzzy fleece blanket, the other with more water, and saw him toward a couch at the back of the room.

As they walked, he caught a glimpse of soft floral chiffon in autumn colors, hair that wasn't quite strawberry blond.

No way. His brain must be little lust-addled, because this might have been a class and all kind of impersonal, but it had still involved a good-looking woman ordering him to hold still while she did devilish things to him with a whip. There was no way he'd just caught a glimpse of Stella here.

He turned his head, looked again, but whomever he'd seen—certainly not his piano teacher—was gone. He didn't think the room wasn't so packed someone could have just vanished into the crowd, and she hadn't been near the door. That convinced him he'd imagined the whole thing.

Unless she'd slipped away toward the restrooms in the far corner, the doors concealed by another set of screens.

Possible, but unlikely.

He took a healthy bite of the cookie and concentrated on putting one foot in front of another. Definitely his imagination had gotten the better of him.

But it would certainly add something to his fantasies, and give him extra incentive to practice.

*

The occasional distracting fantasy or not, everything went fine until Christmas happened.

Paul's family had always been all about Christmas, and his sister-in-law had embraced the celebrations with just as much enthusiasm, adding her own traditions to the mix. Caroling, presents, an advent calendar of a different activity every day, and baked goods…oh, so many baked goods. With both sets of parents, siblings, and a passel of kids from both sides all in the area, it was a multi-day extravaganza. That didn't even take into account friends' festivities, and this was the year that everyone decided a holiday party was the best idea ever.

Bottom line was that Paul's diligence at regular piano practice crashed and burned. He wasn't prepared for his first post-holiday lesson with Stella.

She'd had him working on a longer piece with several movements, and while he'd nailed the beginning, there was a stretch in the center that still caught him up. Several measures started on the offbeat, and rhythm had so far been his weakest point in his lessons. He'd practiced that morning, the first time in a good week, and knew he wasn't going to be ready.

In the happy haze of holiday bliss, he'd assumed she'd cut him some slack.

In that sense, he was an idiot.

She'd bordered the windows of the studio with tiny multicolored LED lights, the same as the ones around the her house. In between hung sparkling ornaments shaped like musical instruments: hunting horns, harps, drums. The Christmas cactus he'd given her at the beginning of the holidays—because he knew how much she loved flowers—sat on a small wooden chest next to the piano where she stored sheet music, blooming lush, hot pink flowers.

The first time he bungled the second movement, she wound the metronome atop the piano and set it into motion. It was an old one, but lovingly cared for, the wood dark and polished, the brass pendulum gleaming. Because staying on beat was his biggest issue, he'd grown to dislike the thing.

The second time he bungled the second movement—in the very same place—she didn't ask him to try again.

She stopped the metronome with one finger. Her lips thinned, deepening the creases around her mouth, the ones he found unbearably sexy. Despite his fears, his cock twitched. He craved her approval, and now his mind flashed to all the delicious fantasies of what she'd require him to do to regain that approval.

She took a piece of art from the wall: a flat, wooden eighth note with piano keys etched on it. It had been hanging near the piano for as long as he'd been taking lessons, and he'd never thought it fit her style, which meant it was probably a gift from a student. The base of the note was about the size of a ping pong paddle, and the stem was the perfect size for gripping.

Now he looked at it in a different way entirely.

"What are you going to do, rap my knuckles with that?" he asked, with more bravado than he felt.

"Don't be ridiculous," she said. "I would never do anything that might damage someone's hands." She tapped the paddle against her palm, a slow, steady rhythm. "Stand up, Mr. Nabholz, place your hands on the top of the piano, and bend over."

Paul's body sprang to obey even while his mind gaped in confusion. Had she actually been at that demo last month, or had she just read his body language, how he reacted to her praise and corrections? In either case, weren't they supposed to talk about this, negotiate a bit?

The hell with that, with all the rules. This was a thousand times hotter, more visceral. And it might not fit the "sane" part of "safe, sane, and consensual," but two out of three wasn't bad: he trusted she'd play safe and he was certainly consenting.

He took a deep breath, then let it out as leaned forward.

The top of the piano was cool under his hands, the varnish silky. It smelled vaguely of lemon and chemicals, as if it had been polished recently. In his line of sight, the drapes were open just enough to allow a glimpse of scruffy suburban woods, gray and brown, mottled in a few spots by patches of dirty snow. Paul focused on those little details, not because he cared about them, but because they grounded him. If he closed his eyes, he might soar too quickly and detach the way he sometimes had playing at a club or party with a near-stranger, turn this all into a fantasy that had little to do with him and Stella, and music, and correction, and maybe even connection. If he dared to glance at Stella, though, see her holding that eighth-note paddle, he'd lose all control.

He would before long anyway. Too many fantasies and dreams were coming together in this little room. But he was determined not to disgrace himself, not to disappoint Stella in this as he had with his music.

Stella moved closer, her low-heeled boots clicking softly on the hardwood floor. He braced himself for a blow he both feared and craved. Instead, she bent over him, arching her body over his in a way that seemed both provocative and protective. The heat of her body seared into him even through the layers of clothes suited to a damp New England winter day. Her perfume—light flowers and herbs with a warm hint of leather—embraced him. His heart raced, but somehow his breathing was slowing to match the rhythm of hers.

Oh, he could close his eyes this time. No way in hell he'd lose track of the sweet, scary reality of Stella.

She reached for the metronome, pulled it closer. Then she leaned closer and whispered in his ear, "Don't think of this as a punishment, Mr. Nabholz. Think of it as an instructional technique uniquely suited to your interests. But you'll need to hold very still." He couldn't see her face well, but he swore he could *hear* her devious, sexy smile. "I know you can do that." Her voice was lower, husky. "I saw how well you did for Mistress Marlene and her whip."

With one flick of her hand, she set the metronome ticking. That damn beat, the one he kept losing, ticked out relentlessly as the little brass pendulum swung back and forth.

Adagio ma non troppo, slow but not too slow, it said on the sheet music—wording that left a lot of room for confusion.

She struck as the metronome ticked, a firm blow that sent bright pain vibrating through his ass. The pain was just starting to morph into sharp, hot pleasure when the metronome and Stella struck again. Jarring, but my God, so good. So right. That heat, that pain that wasn't exactly pain, washed over him again, and this time it stroked along his nerve endings. His balls tightened. His dick, already half-hard, swelled. He didn't exactly have time to enjoy the sensation, though, before the metronome and Stella did their evil work at precisely the same time.

After a few more perfectly timed swats, Paul's ass throbbed and pleasure and pain were mingling in a way that went to his head like good Scotch—and to his cock like sweet sin, like all his masturbatory fantasies of Stella come to red-hot life, only better because of the specificity, the realness. Stella's perfume, lemon polish, the gray day outside, the insistent ticking of the metronome marking when the next blow would fall.

And the equally insistent tick in his own brain that now warned him.

Not so he could get away. He wouldn't do that, even if the pain had been harsher, not diffusing to pleasure so readily. She'd told him to bend over. Told him to hold still.

He hadn't been a good student for her over the holidays, but he was going to be good for her now if it killed him. And it might—with pleasure.

Thank goodness the movement he'd bungled wasn't a fast one. Adagio ma non troppo was quite rapid enough—though some perverse part of him couldn't help wondering how it would feel with a faster piece that allowed no recovery time.

Oh lord. Brutally hot. How it would feel was brutally hot.

He mentally shook himself. Focus on the moment. Focus on the point Stella was imprinting onto his skin. Focus on pleasing her right here and now, not some phantom scene.

Focus on the rhythm of this mix of pleasure and pain, a rhythm that pulsed throughout his body now. His cock, of course, but everywhere that blood flowed, everywhere he had nerve endings. It was in his fingers now, and he'd never forget that rhythm again.

Which was her point, he supposed.

His throbbing cock and aching balls almost didn't care what her point was.

Almost. Because this wouldn't be nearly as sweet without her will, her intention, behind it, shaping him, if only in a small, specific way.

Thinking about that, thinking of her hand and will acting in concert to correct him, almost pushed him to the edge.

He bit his lip, thought about doing taxes, and gingerly raised one hand from the gleaming surface of the piano. "Stella...my lady...I'm close. Really close."

He swore he could hear her evil grin as she said, "So am I. Two more measures. Count."

The *don't come* was implied.

He counted and, thanks to the muse Euterpe, he did so correctly. The concentration helped him hold off the orgasm that threatened.

This time, she walked around the piano to shut off the metronome. Maybe she realized that leaning over him teasingly, as she had before, would slay him. Her hand brushing his came damn close to doing so.

"Now," she said casually, as if none of this had happened, as she hung the eighth note back on the wall, "let's try the second movement again."

Was she serious? Paul stared at her, struggling to find words to speak through the haze of desire. "I don't think..." he finally managed, and helplessly gestured at his crotch.

Her cool blue gaze flicked down, and she took in the bulge in his pants. He'd wept so much precome, it had soaked through his underwear and left a dark stain on his khakis.

He'd never been so hard before, and that erection wasn't going away anytime soon. If she asked him to leave, he would, but he didn't have the presence of mind to drive safely.

He hoped beyond hope that she wouldn't ask him to leave.

"Then I suggest you take care of that," she said, nodding toward the bathroom.

The studio had a tiny facility, just barely big enough to hold a toilet and sink. Paul's lankiness meant his knees hit the door when he sat.

He nodded and shuffled into the little room, his ass on fire and his cock steely hard. Inside, his hands shook with need as he fumbled with the button of his khakis and eased his underwear down over his purpled cock.

There was hand lotion on the edge of the small sink, something with a light, floral scent that reminded him of Stella, and his erection surged again as he pumped the lotion into his palm. He knew it would take only a few strokes before he blew.

Was she listening outside the door? Had paddling him made her wet; was seeing his reaction to her turning her on? Would she want him to pleasure her, or didn't he have her approval for that yet?

He didn't know, and none of it really mattered. He knew, instinctively, that she was waiting for him to finish, and he knew better than to keep Stella waiting.

Wrapping his lotion-slick fingers around his cock, he squeezed, pumped. Closed his eyes and saw Stella. He couldn't stop the groan that wrenched out of him as he came, and black spots like musical notes danced in his vision.

When he emerged from the bathroom, Stella was paging through some sheet music. She looked up. "All set?"

He nodded, and very carefully eased himself down on the piano bench.

She didn't set the metronome in motion, and he didn't need her to. His ass throbbed rhythmically, reminding him every second—and this time, he played the movement perfectly.

This time she nodded her approval, a small smile on her pink lips, and his cock twitched again.

*

For the next week, Paul needed some quality alone time with his right hand and a lot of lube before he even attempted to practice that piece. But he did practice it, religiously. He arrived at his lesson with his body taut and quivering as the strings on a violin.

Stella's smiles were warmer than he remembered and she occasionally looked at him with an expression that suggested her thoughts were as naughty as some of his. But she didn't touch him except for one slim, pink-nailed finger coming to rest on his shoulder when he demonstrated he could now play the troublesome piece at the correct tempo and even with a little flair. But instead of saying "Nice job" or "Well done," she said "Good boy," as a domme might say to her sub when he pleased her.

That was enough to send him off with a spring in his step and a determination to conquer the new piece she'd given him to take home and practice. She hadn't played it for him this time or given him a chance to run through it and get feedback. They'd run short on time and this was one of the rare Tuesday afternoons someone had the 3 p.m. slot, doing a make-up lesson or something.

But he'd figure it out.

Or he wouldn't.

It would be a win either way.

*

Much as he liked a good paddling, Paul decided he'd prefer it as a reward than a punishment, with those sweet pink lips shaping "Good boy" (which they did in his fantasies, before those sweet pink lips shaped themselves around a needy part of his anatomy). So he practiced like crazy. He even found a YouTube video of someone playing the piece, though the professional pianist added all kinds of flourishes to dress up what Paul was pretty sure was supposed to be a simple early 20th-century art song.

He had this. He had this down cold.

Until Stella smiled at him and a glint of mischief broke through her attempt to look like his friendly piano teacher and nothing more.

Then a certain percentage of blood left his brain to inhabit his dick. He sat down at the piano as soon as he could, hoping to hide the twitch in his trousers.

But he had a feeling she'd noticed.

He started the song off well enough, hitting all the right notes, sticking to what he hoped was the correct tempo. But all the time Stella was studying him and maybe it was no more than she used to do, but to his fevered brain, she was a predator watching her prey. His cock got harder and harder, while his brain got progressively foggier.

And his playing got faster and sloppier.

"That's enough for now." Stella's voice cut through the fog in his brain enough that he stopped playing. Enough that he realized he'd made a mess of the piece and felt bad for disappointing both himself and Stella.

But not so bad his cock didn't finish springing to painful attention in anticipation of what might come.

She set the Christmas cactus on the floor and opened the top of the chest. He hadn't realized there was a compartment at the top; he'd noticed only the drawers for sheet music. She pulled out an off-white canvas, which she draped over the front of the piano, catching it in the lid on top and letting it hang down, covering the keys.

"Remove your pants and underwear," she said.

Again, no discussion; he chose to trust her. He slipped off his shoes and socks, and did as she asked, folding his pants neatly because he imagined she'd want him to. When she told him to stand and put his hands on the piano, he did, wondering if she'd paddle him with the wooden eighth note again, or use her hand, or some other implement he hadn't noticed in the room.

Instead, she removed a bottle of lube from the cabinet and drizzled some into her hand. His already insistent cock twitched in anticipation…of what, he didn't particularly care. So many decadent things started with lube—although if she were going to unearth a strap-on from inside the piano bench, he'd have expected her to do it before smearing her hand with lube. Stella was meticulous. One of her charms, as far as Paul was concerned; part of her aura of precision and control.

"You were doing well at first, considering we didn't have a chance to review it together last week. But then you got distracted." She glanced in an obvious way at this straining cock. "And we're going to have to deal with that before you can focus on music again."

She continued, "I'll take this as an opportunity to reinforce the correct tempo for this piece—which is slow. You're constantly rushing the beat. You'll hear recordings where it's played at lightning speed and dressed up, but you have to be a virtuoso *and* know the piece the way you know your own breathing to pull that off. Not many people can become virtuosi, but I can help you know this piece, and its tempo, in your flesh and blood."

"Thank you." He wasn't entirely sure what he was thanking her for, not yet, but it seemed like the right thing to say.

She reached around him, leaning over his body far more than necessary as she had the day of the paddling. He swore he felt her burning through her pale blue cashmere sweater and full, calf-length gray wool skirt. But as soon as she flicked the metronome on, she drew away from him.

Only to stand next to him and place her well-slicked hand onto his throbbing dick. He tensed, both from the shock of pleasure at her touch and from lust-addled bewilderment. He'd fantasized about this (among other things) for weeks, but now that it was actually happening, he wasn't sure how to react, what to do or say. It seemed impossible.

"You're rushing the beat," Stella repeated. "So pay attention to it. Thrust in time to this beat, and this beat only. If you speed up, we'll stop immediately. If you slow down, we'll stop immediately. Maintain the rhythm. Begin."

His hips moved automatically, well before his brain had time to process the command.

Forward thrust through the vise of her hand, feeling the caress over the sensitive head, back again, with the pinnacle of each forward or backward motion timed to the beat of the metronome.

If this was the tempo the composer had intended, that pianist on YouTube had been playing it about four times too fast. That was his last truly coherent thought for a while.

Apparently his body was better at taking orders, and thank goodness for that, because the glorious sensation of her cock sliding between the warm, slick tunnel of her lubed fingers destroyed any hope his brain had of conscious thought.

If this was the tempo at Stella insisted he move, Paul was going to lose his mind from pleasure and frustration. After only a couple of measures, his body was on fire, and not long after that, his mind started to slip into that still, centered place where all that mattered was Stella and him and this moment. His heart raced, far faster than the pace of the metronome, but the blood pounding in his cock kept perfect time. He rode the bliss, rode the exquisite pleasure of her touch, tried to surf them to a place where his own climax didn't matter, only pleasing her.

But he was too far gone, had been too far gone as soon as she told him to undress. The piece wasn't all that long, but he was going to reach his climax long before it did.

He wouldn't rush the beat, though. He knew better, no matter how desperately he wanted to. A few quick jerks would easily bring him over the edge, no matter how quickly she let go—but he dimly knew that would disappoint Stella. And disappointing her would erase the pleasure of orgasm.

"Please," he said through clenched teeth. "I need..."

"I know. Just hold out for four more measures."

Four measures. Twelve excruciating, delicious strokes, timed to music that wasn't actually playing, but he could hear now in the rush of his blood.

Then she said, as calmly as she might say, "Play that again," Stella said, "Come for me. That's a good boy."

And he did, without speeding up or slowing down, on that very last beat before he froze. The noises he made were their own kind of music, rough and primal, as he spasmed and shot helplessly onto the canvas covering the piano for what seemed a lifetime of unbelievable pleasure, his cock pulsing in the hot vise of Stella's fingers.

For a moment all he could do was hang his head onto his outstretched arms and struggle to keep standing on legs that had turned to water. The metronome stopped, and he managed to whisper "Thank you" into the ensuing silence.

He heard Stella move to the tiny restroom, heard the water run as she her hands. Heard her boots clicking on the floor as she returned.

He knew what to do without being told. He grabbed his clothes, went to the bathroom himself, cleaned himself up. Wiping the lube from his cock with a rose-colored washcloth made him half-hard again as he flashed back to what had just happened. He soaked the cloth in cold water, and by sheer force of will convinced himself to go flaccid. Otherwise he wouldn't be able to play, and that would disappoint her, and the thought of disappointing her sent a wave of panic through him.

When he finally got to play the piece, he still fumbled a few notes, but the timing was in the beat of his blood. He didn't rush the beat once, not once. He wasn't even tempted to.

And after he played for her, she said, "Well done," and her voice conveyed the sincerity of her words. He felt himself flush with pride, and was almost relieved that the blood had gone up to his face rather than down to his pants.

Although in truth, the flush consumed his entire body, spreading out through his groin as well.

"Thank you," he said again.

A smile played across her lush pink lips, and something glittered in those blue-green eyes. "I'd say you get a reward, but it seems you've already received one."

"The reward is in the music," he said, almost without thinking, but as soon as the concept left his lips he knew it was true, knew it with a startling clarity and deep peace.

Warmth flooded her expression. "If only one student says that to me, I know I've done my job," she said.

"You inspire your students," he said.

One corner of her mouth lifted in a wicked grin. "And occasionally a student inspires me," she said, and he knew she wasn't talking about the musical instruction—at least, not exactly.

*

They never spoke about their extracurricular sessions. Strange, but somehow Paul didn't want to break the spell by changing the...well, the rhythm.

The "corrections" were simply a part of his musical education, just like the warm-ups he did, scales and the like, at the beginning of each lesson, or how she would demonstrate a particularly complex new skill he hadn't encountered yet.

That made it somehow all the more thrilling. The inscrutable domme. He couldn't read her, and it wasn't his place to question her, and that *worked*.

Once, when she produced a crop, he winced when she hit the same spot one too many times and requested she back off, remembering her words from the first time they met, about undue pain and damage. Now, she obliged, and praised him for speaking up.

He trusted her. He lusted for her. And he let her lead the relationship—if what was going on could even be called a relationship—in the way she saw fit.

In large part due to her, music became an even bigger part of his life. He'd told her he'd always wanted to play piano, and that was true, but he hadn't even realized himself how much truth there was in it. The more he played, the more he craved it. Which was true of both their relationship and music, really.

He joined a country-rock band, playing mostly covers, but a few original pieces as well, including two he'd written. The guys in the band were all musicians, but none of them, including Paul, had any real desire for fame and fortune. The strong local following they had was enough, because it allowed them opportunities to play, and that was what they all loved to do.

Paul had replaced their previous keyboardist, and once he was up to speed, they scheduled their first gig with him. Stella knew about the project, of course; he'd told her as soon as he'd joined, and she'd helped him learn the trickier aspects of some of the songs. So he naturally invited her to the first gig, and she said she'd be delighted.

Even so, a part of him hadn't really expected her to come.

He'd looked for her before they started, one eye on the crowd while he made sure his gear was set up properly. Once they began playing, he was focused on the music—or so he told himself.

He was still instantly aware the moment she entered the room.

The establishment, in nearby Waltham, could best be described as a dive bar. Low-ceilinged and dark even with all the lights on, it held maybe a hundred people, and if it did, that was probably in violation of the occupancy code. The bar stretched along one wall across from the stage, if a platform less than a foot high and barely big enough for the band members to crowd onto could be called a stage. (The lead guitar and bass players often stepped off the sides to have more room to jam.) There was no room for a dance floor among the crowded-together round tables and stools.

There was a sense that the bar was smoky even though smoking laws had come into effect years ago. Maybe it was just the haze of patrons past and present. At the beginning of the night, the space smelled like floor polish and the beef grilling in the kitchen for nachos; by an hour in, it smelled like spilled beer and aftershave. Talking was impossible when the band was playing, even though they had their amps turned down so they didn't blast listeners right out of the room. Between sets, there was a cacophony of conversation and drink orders.

Despite how crowded it was, Stella managed to find a seat at the bar, about as far away from the stage as you could get in the room (i.e., not very far), which was probably the best spot acoustically speaking.

Paul would have recognized her anywhere just by the way she moved, even though tonight she was dressed differently than he'd ever seen her. In keeping with the atmosphere, she had on faded jeans and a soft, many-times-washed grey concert tee. Low-heeled lace-up black boots; a jacket slung over one arm. From this distance, he couldn't make out the band logo on the T-shirt, but he wasn't really trying. His sight was filled with the way the simple garments caressed her body, clinging in the right places without being tight, accentuating her gentle curves without being blatant. The outfit was far, far sexier than the miniskirts and down-to-there vee necks on many of the women here.

He lost himself in the joy of playing music, even as he knew she ordered a drink, even as he wished the straw between her pink lips was his cock. He never stopped being aware of her, to the point of believing he could smell that floral scent she always wore, even as he wove the keyboard melodies with the guitar and bass and drums, becoming part of the unit. He knew when she clapped when a song finished; he knew when a delicate line creased the space between her brows as she listened to the interplay of instruments in a way few others in the bar had the ability to do.

He never stopped being half-hard, either.

When they finished for the night, he packed up his equipment, set it by the back door, then walked through the lingering crowd.

More than one woman blatantly eyed him as he went by, their gazes lingering on his crotch, then raising to his face in invitation. He gave each one a short nod because he truly appreciated they'd come to hear the band play, but they were ghosts compared to the reality of Stella.

She handed him a glass of water, a lemon slice tucked along the rim. "Well done!" she said. "You've found an excellent group of musicians. I could tell how much joy you all have for performing."

"Thanks," he said. "It's a blast—playing with a group, being a part of how the different instruments join together to become a greater whole, is exhilarating."

She took his right hand, her soft thumb running over the scars. "You've exceeded my expectations as a student," she admitted.

His breath caught. It was as intimate a thing as she'd ever said to him. He wasn't sure how to respond, so he took the coward's route: avoidance. "I screwed up a few times."

Something steely flashed in her blue-green eyes. "Well, there is that," she said. "You and your rhythm issues. You rushed the beat in two songs, and came in late after the bridge in another."

He nodded, his mouth dry despite the water he'd been sipping.

She tilted her head. "I think that's something we should work on, then, don't you?"

His groin flooded with heat; his cock throbbed, aching for her touch. His ass clenched at the memory of the sweet release of pain she could inflict, pain he craved.

"I'm scheduled for a lesson on Tuesday," he said. It was Saturday night now. Tuesday seemed as far away as next Christmas.

"I was thinking of tonight," she said, and his legs turned to water even as his heart pounded a sudden strong beat—not rushing, not lagging—in his chest.

He drove through the darkness, followed her car a few exits up the highway and down the familiar, quiet streets of Lexington. When he parked and got out of his car, she was waiting for him on the herringbone brick of her front walk, at the intersection where the path went around the side of the house and back to the studio.

Without speaking, she held out her hand. Without speaking, he took it.

She led him, for the first time, into her house.

Author of *Out of the Frying Pan*

Sophie MOUETTE

CAT SCRATCH FEVER

"This is a delightful, amusing
and sexy whodunit."
– *Romantic Times*

Turn the page for a sexy taste of
Sophie Mouette's sizzling-hot novel
Cat Scratch Fever,
available now at your favorite retailer.

Cat Scratch Fever

"Katherine," Valerie said. Just a name, but she could feel its weight on her tongue, the intention giving it the force of some ritual greeting.

"My lady."

Katherine, so confident at work, in this setting became almost inaudible.

The shy whisper sent a thrill through Valerie. She'd had some delightful boys who'd been her play-partners. But oh, nothing had ever compared to the pleasure of seeing Katherine kneeling before her.

And it was strange because Valerie wasn't normally that interested in women (men had always seemed more entertaining to hurt and then comfort afterward) or in people who turned their submission on and off like a faucet. Katherine was unquestionably female, and in most contexts you'd think she didn't have a yielding bone in her body. But that made it all the more exciting when she did give up control.

Valerie crossed the room to her in a few brisk strides. She circled the kneeling woman slowly, once and then again. She never took her eyes off of Katherine and maintained eye contact as much as was physically possible.

At first, Katherine seemed far away, lost in thought rather than lost in lust, the corners of her mouth tight. As

Valerie started a third pass, though, she saw that Katherine was trembling slightly. Her eyes were wide, pupils hiding so much of the grey iris that she looked like some frightened nocturnal creature.

Prey.

It was one thing to see that look on the face of someone you'd always known as a sub, someone you'd met through the scene. That was sweet in its own right, especially when you could get him to go just a little deeper than he ever had before. But seeing it on the face of someone who knew as much about big-cat genetics as anyone on the planet, someone who'd built a remarkable organization starting from nothing but a vision, someone usually described by words such as tough, driven, and fearless...

It was hard to say if the thrill started in her mind and worked its way to her groin or vice versa, but it seemed to hit every key point in between. Her nipples, suddenly sensitive—which didn't usually happen until a scene was well under-way. Her skin, tingling with excitement. Her hands, aching to touch, stroke, slap.

And maybe her heart, too, because she found herself not-ing the circles under Katherine's eyes and feeling a surge of anger. If Katherine were losing sleep, it should be because she was desperate with lust, not desperate for funding. Maybe it was time to do something more to help out.

She had a few ideas. But meanwhile, she could take both their minds off mundane matters for a while.

She was behind Katherine now, out of her easy line of sight. Quick as a hunting cat, Valerie reached out, buried her fingers in the disordered mop of red curls at the nape of Katherine's neck and pulled her head back.

Katherine leaned with the motion, creating a lovely backward arch to her body. Holding her in position, Valerie bent and gave her a hard, claiming kiss, biting at her lower lip. It was awkward, not a position either could sustain for long, but it made the point.

If Katherine's expression was to believed when Valerie relaxed her grip slightly, it made the point very well indeed.

"Get up," she ordered, giving a tug on Katherine's hair to emphasize the point. She did, although with a certain hesitation that probably came from trying to figure out how best to stand without looking too awkward. Something to work on in future. Valerie did like her toys to move elegantly and Katherine was athletic enough that it should be easy enough to teach her. But meanwhile...

Smack!

Her hand felt better for having connected with Katherine's bottom. "When I tell you to do something, do it immediately," she barked, sounding far more harsh than she felt. She wasn't annoyed. She wouldn't have touched Katherine if she had been. She played at punishment with Katherine, but the redhead, though a masochist, was definitely not slavish, and she hadn't given Valerie the right to punish her for real.

And this wouldn't have merited real punishment even if punishment had been part of the rules; her awkwardness was far too cute. If anything, Valerie was delighted to have the excuse to give them both a taste of the pleasures to come later in the evening.

Katherine caught on to that immediately. She nodded and mouthed, "I'm sorry, my lady," but her eyes were sparkling. She still had a bit of that prey-animal look, but the kind of fear she showed was the kind only humans seemed to feel, the enjoyable kind induced by horror movies or amusement-park rides.

Katherine carried her own Stephen King and Disneyland with her. And Valerie had the key.

"You don't seem very contrite."

Katherine seemed unsure what to do. On the one hand, she knew how the game was played. On the other hand, after the sort of day she'd probably had, she must desperately need the release that only pain seemed to offer her. Valerie could almost see Katherine's mind weighing the options, trying to figure out whether she'd get what she needed faster by behaving or misbehaving.

Valerie would never let on that she'd get it equally fast either way. Oh, there were plans for later, delicious plans for pain and pleasure that built slowly and sensually to a crescendo. But Katherine wasn't the only one who was itching for some stress release.

While Katherine still hesitated, she grabbed her and pushed her toward a low leather chair. "Take off your clothes and bend over."

"What? We're in the living room!" Now there was a hint of real rebellion in Katherine's voice. Katherine was rather modest for a lady with her inclinations.

Valerie lowered her voice to a deep, menacing purr. "Yes, we are, my dear. And I just told you to take your clothes off. I'm waiting. And you know how impatient I am."

"But…"

"Do it!"

Valerie wouldn't have believed Katherine's eyes could get any wider, but they did. She seemed to have trouble with her buttons and the buckle of her belt.

Valerie didn't bother to hide her smile when Katherine stood naked before her. Clothes were purely functional for Katherine; she wore jeans or khaki shorts and tees when she could get away with being casual, and basic pantsuits when something more formal was required. And she tended to buy everything a little large. The result was that seeing her naked was always astonishing.

She had a body like a '50s pinup—generous, soft breasts, a tiny waist flaring to rather wide hips, and a round, spankable bottom. Her legs were a little short in proportion and a little full in the thigh, but well-muscled. Skin of warm ivory was sprinkled liberally with golden-brown freckles. Not a fashionable look right now, but that just confirmed Valerie's opinion that most people weren't too bright.

Valerie noted that the red curls on her mons had been trimmed to a neat strip, the lips apparently shaved. Good—that had been phrased as a request and Katherine had been perceptive enough (or eager enough for a possible reward) to follow it as if it were an order. It was hard to tell, but it looked as though she was getting pouty from excitement, despite her protests.

For a moment longer than she should have, Katherine stood as if frozen under Valerie's gaze. Her eyes never left Valerie's, but they seemed unfocused. Her breathing was fast and shallow.

Again, prey.

Then she seemed to remember what her orders were, turned, and bent over the chair.

Valerie decided not to complain about that bit of hesitation. She'd feel like a hypocrite; she'd been enjoying the view far too much.

This view, though, was even better, accenting the ample, heart-shaped ass, the curve of the spine that showed Katherine's submission. Her legs were slightly parted, allowing Valerie to see how slick she was starting to get.

Excellent. This worked nicely into Valerie's continuing quest to see just how many times, and how many ways, she could make Katherine come without direct genital contact.

Spanking usually worked. And that beautiful ass was looking much too pale.

Smack! Keeping the appearance of punishment for Katherine's earlier rebellion, she started in without any warm-up, giving a good, hard slap right off.

Katherine let out a shriek, but the way she rolled her hips told Valerie that she'd enjoyed it despite, or maybe because of, the initial shock. She let her hand linger a bit on the warm, resilient skin, however, gauging the reaction a little longer before continuing, breathing in Katherine's smell. (Sunscreen, a light perfume of green apples and vanilla, the musk of an aroused woman. And something warm and wild, like sun-warmed fur—even if Katherine had spent most of her day trapped at her desk, she always seemed to carry a hint of the cats with her.)

Katherine's breath was already a bit more ragged, a combination of excitement and working through the sudden, sharp pain. But she didn't appear to be in any distress, judging from her Mona Lisa smile.

The next blows fell in a flurry, not giving Katherine time to process them or to catch her breath. Valerie wasn't holding back. Her own palm was pink and stinging, but she didn't care. Katherine's reddened ass, her noises that blended ecstasy and pain, the way she'd flinch away and then arch back, all conspired to arouse her as well. She'd meant to give ten and stop, a tease to both of them, but the reactions were just too exquisite. She kept going, sometimes staccato, sometimes with slow deliberateness.

Her own sex seemed to pulse with the blows, or maybe with Katherine's reactions to them. She wondered if they were throbbing in rhythm.

Moisture was trickling down Katherine's thighs now. Her pussy lips were swollen, visibly twitching. Clearly she was ready to come from just a little more attention. She must have needed this session even more than Valerie had suspected—she didn't usually react so fast.

Valerie stopped.

She stroked her hands along Katherine's trembling body. Although the room was air-conditioned to a pleasant temperature, the redhead was lightly glazed in sweat, releasing more of that delicious combination of civilized cologne and wild feline. Her eyes, too, looked glazed.

"Still with me?" Valerie whispered.

A nod showed that Katherine still understood simple English sentences.

"Good. I'm going to give you five more and on the fifth I want you to come. Do you understand?"

Another small nod.

Katherine made it to three.

Then she threw her head up and howled. No pain in there now, just ecstasy. Her hips twitched and bucked. Then she slumped bonelessly forward, sprawling over the arm of the chair in a position only particularly relaxed cats could normally achieve.

"Good girl," Valerie murmured, kneeling down beside the chair and gathering Katherine into her arms as best she could. "That's my good little pain slut. Is that better now?"

Katherine looked up. Her grey eyes weren't very focused, but it was post-orgasmic haze now. Pain always relaxed her. "Better? It's so much better I don't even remember what was wrong before!" she exclaimed. Then she began to giggle.

Another job well done. Now they'd have dinner, a little wine, and then they'd start again.

She wondered how Katherine would react when she learned she'd be eating dinner naked on the deck....

About the Author

Author of the 4-star (*Romantic Times*) novel *Cat Scratch Fever, Out of the Frying Pan, Possessed, Undressed, and in a Mess,* and many short stories, Sophie Mouette is the brainchild of two widely published authors of erotica, romance, and speculative fiction.

The two halves of Sophie—Dayle A. Dermatis (aka Andrea Dale) and Teresa Noelle Roberts—met more than two decades ago at a writers' conference. Talking nonstop, they closed down the hotel bar and went somewhere else to keep on talking. Although they've always lived on opposite sides of the country (and for a few years, on opposite sides of the Atlantic), they've remained very close friends, and it was only natural that they should start writing together as well.

Visit SophieMouette.com for more information.